Messy Potatoes

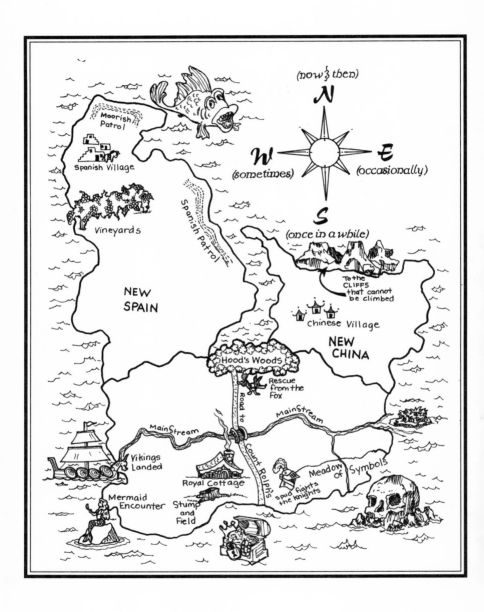

The King of Messy Potatoes

To Justin:
Best wishes,

BY

JOHN DASHNEY

John Dashney

2007

SEATTLE, WASHINGTON

1997

STORM PEAK PRESS
157 YESLER WAY, SUITE 413
SEATTLE, WASHINGTON 98104

© 1997, JOHN DASHNEY

ISBN 0-9641357-6-0

LIBRARY OF CONGRESS CATALOG CARD NUMBER: 97-68559

DEDICATED TO THE DESCENDANTS OF

THOMAS S. BROOKS
&
SUSAN M. KNEALE

Chapter One

Most of this happened back in the 1980's when I was a kid. But some of it happened way before I was born, and some of the things that happened to Spud might not have happened at all.

But maybe they did. I hope they did.

My name is John Kneale Brooks. Most of the time people call me Jack. Kneale was Mom's last name before she married Dad. It's pronounced "kneel"—like when you go down on your knees—but it has this funny spelling because it's a Manx name.

When I was six, I met Grandfather Kneale for the second time. I don't remember the first time because I was only two months old. Mom has a picture of it, though. It shows Grandfather holding me and looking very serious. I'm all wrapped up in a white bundle and have my mouth wide open. Mom says I was screaming blue murder because Grandfather had just splashed cold water over me. It's called being baptized.

Grandfather Kneale was an Episcopal priest. In the picture he is all dressed up in fancy robes that make him look like a king without a crown. Mom and Dad are standing on either side of him. Grandma and Grandpa Brooks stand next to Dad, and next to Mom is a lady I never got to meet.

She was Grandmother Kneale, and she died from a stroke just a month after the picture was taken.

When she died, Grandfather gave up his church job and became a professor in a college where they train Episcopal priests. I learned it was called a seminary. A year later he left for somewhere in the Middle East to do research for a book he wanted to write. It would be called *The Kings of Mesopotamia*.

He didn't know it then, but he was actually going to write two books. I was the reason he wrote the second one.

But all that happened later. For the first six years of my life I never thought of him as a grandfather, the way I did with Grandpa Brooks. In fact, I never really thought of him at all. To me he was just the man in the picture, dressed in those robes that made him look like a king without a crown.

He'd send presents at Christmas or on my birthday. The packages had strange stamps and funny writing on them. Usually they held coins or stuff to wear. There weren't many toys. Mom said it was because he was out in the field in a poor part of the country, and there weren't any stores for shopping.

Then one spring Grandfather Kneale came home. I was finishing kindergarten and could read just a little, so Mom showed me his letter. It was in cursive, but at the bottom he had carefully printed a message for me.

"Jack, I hope you will come visit me this summer," it said.

I wasn't sure if I liked the idea or not. Spending time with Grandpa and Grandma meant going to see Grandpa and Grandma Brooks in their house on the other side of town. There would always be one or two cousins there, too. Dad had five brothers and sisters, so I had lots of cousins on that side of the family.

But Mom had grown up as an only child. I asked her once why she didn't have any brothers or sisters. She looked sad for a moment, then she said, "I had one brother, but he died a long time ago."

"Before I was born?" I asked.

"Before you were born and before I was born," she said.

"Would he have been my uncle then?" I asked. I wasn't too sure yet about which relatives were called what.

"Yes. His name was Hugh. He would have liked you."

I wasn't sure how she knew that. After all, she had never seen him either. And I wasn't sure if I wanted to visit Grandfather Kneale. So I asked the question I always used whenever I needed time to think.

"But why?"

"Why not?" she answered. "You're a likable kid." She gathered me up in a big hug, and I knew the argument was over before I could get it started. But I still wasn't sure about staying with Grandfather Kneale.

"Does he live way far away?" I asked.

"Two or three hours by car," she said. "It's not like the other side of the world where he did his research."

But I had no idea then of how big the world was. Two or three hours by car could well have been clear over on the other side of the globe, for all I knew.

"Why does he want to see me?" I asked suspiciously.

"Because you are his only grandchild and he loves you very much," she said.

I tried again. "Does he have a nice house?"

"Yes. It's the same house where I grew up. Hugh was a boy there, too. He rented it to some students while he was gone. A lady named Mrs. Phelps keeps it clean and cooks for him, but she doesn't live there." She smiled and added, "It's a big old house with lots of rooms to explore. Trust me. You'll like it."

It looked like I was going, whether I wanted to or not. But I still had one more excuse to try.

"There won't be anyone to play with!"

"Mrs. Phelps has a grandson about your age," Mom said, "and Bill and Tami will be with Grandma and Grandpa Brooks next month while your Aunt Nora has another baby. You told me just last week that you don't like them."

That was true enough. My cousin Bill was bigger and older, and he liked to pick on me whenever Grandma wasn't looking, which was most of the time. Tami was a little pest who followed me around and whined all day. If they were going to be with Grandma and Grandpa Brooks for a whole month, then Grandfather Kneale and his big old house began to look better. But I still wasn't sure.

"Can I come right back if I don't like it?" I asked.

Mom shook her head and smiled. "You *will* like it," she said, "and you have to give it a chance. Grandfather Kneale is a wonderful man, once you get to know him. After all, he's *my* dad, and you love me, don't you?"

"Sure I do," I said.

"Then you will love him too," she said in that tone which meant, "This discussion is over."

"When am I going?" I asked without much enthusiasm.

"In a few days," she said. "We'll call him first. You can talk to him on the phone. He may sound a little gruff, but he's a big old teddy bear at heart. And remember, he's a priest too."

"Does that mean he talks to God?" I asked.

"Every day and twice on Sunday." She said it like it was a joke, but I knew she meant it. I started to get curious about this grandfather who dressed in robes that made him look like a king without a crown. Would somebody who talked to God every day and twice on Sunday have time for a six-year-old grandson?

"What was he doing over on the other side of the world?" I asked. I wasn't sure where the other side of the world was, but I'd heard Mom and Dad use the term.

"He was doing research for a book," she said. "Your grandfather teaches at a special college where people study to become priests in the Episcopal Church. His specialty is Old Testament History, and his book will be about the kings of Mesopotamia."

Of course, this meant nothing to me. I had no idea where Mesopotamia was, or even what it was. I couldn't even say it right. We called Grandfather Kneale a few days later to plan the visit. I got to talk to him for a few minutes. His voice was low and musical. He almost seemed to sing the words to me.

"Do you have a big-screen TV?" I asked.

"I don't have any television at all," he answered. "But I will borrow a small one and hook it up for you."

"Are you going to get cable?" I asked without much hope.

"No, but I can rent a tape player and get some movies, if you would like that."

"Mom and Dad only let me watch the G-ones," I said, hoping he might be a little more liberal. He wasn't.

"That's all you'll get here too," he replied. "But we can do other things."

"What kind of other things?" I asked without much hope.

"Well, I used to tell your mother stories when she was a little girl. Has she ever told you about any of them?"

She hadn't. It was hard to picture Mom as a little girl, although I knew she must have been one once. "What kind of stories were they?" I asked him.

"Ones I made up," he said. "I'm surprised she hasn't told any of them to you. Well, I guess I can make up some more."

"Could you tell me about the King of Messy Potatoes?"

"The *what*?"

"You know... the guy you're gonna write the book about."

The line went silent for a few seconds. Then the sound of an enormous chuckle filled my ears. For some reason I thought of an elephant coughing with a mouthful of soup. "The_King_ of_Messy_Potatoes!" He said each word slowly and carefully, like it was a new idea that had just hit him. "What a delightful thought!" he added. "We could do something with that! I'll work on it!"

I passed the phone back to Mom, who made the arrangements and then hung up. "Grandfather told me he used to make up stories for you when you were little," I said.

"That's right," she said with a smile. "I'd forgotten about them. He told me one every night before I went to sleep, because I was afraid of the dark."

"Why didn't you tell any of them to me?"

"Because you never were afraid of the dark," she said. (That's not quite true. I was... just a little.) "Anyway, I can't tell them the way he did. The atmosphere's not right here."

"What do you mean?"

"They were stories about the old times long ago," she explained. "You need a big old house like he has to make them come alive, not this modern thing we live in. I suppose the best place would be a campfire out under the stars."

"Do you think he would take me camping then?" I asked.

She shook her head. "I'm afraid Grandfather Kneale is too old for that now," she said. "You see, he's a lot older than Grandpa Brooks. You'll need to treat him carefully. No rough-housing and no teasing either."

That sure didn't sound like much fun. Grandpa Brooks always wrestled with me, and even Grandma would tease me and rumple my hair. What would we do at Grandfather Kneale's big old house? Was I going to have to be quiet all the time, like at the library?

Mom saw the worried look on my face. "Hey!" she said. "Grandfather Kneale is a wonderful man. You'll love him. Just remember: you love different people in different ways for different reasons."

I wondered how I was supposed to do that. Well, it looked like I was going to find out.

We made the trip a few days later. It must have been on a weekend, because Mom and Dad both came along. But neither of them brought suitcases, so I knew they wouldn't be staying. Mom had packed a bag of clothes and a carton of toys for me.

"One last thing," she said as we left. "Don't ask him anything about Hugh. It would make him feel very bad."

Grandfather Kneale's house wasn't really big, but it was one of those old houses with high ceilings and lots of small rooms, closets and cubbyholes to explore. The furniture had that smell of oldness that comes from years of cleaning, dusting and polishing.

Then I saw him, really saw him, for the first time. My other grandfather, the Reverend Ehric Kneale. But he wasn't wearing robes, so he didn't look at all like a king.

He was tall and unusually thin, and he smelled like the furniture. It wasn't a bad smell. In fact, I sort of liked it. But all the shapes and sounds and smells were different here. It wasn't really spooky, but it was enough to make me nervous.

I noticed the difference in sounds right away. Maybe it was the small rooms with the high ceilings. They seemed to soak up noises, so that the house had the quietness of a church just before the service begins.

Maybe that's why Grandfather Kneale had such a powerful voice. I don't mean that he shouted. He didn't. But whenever he opened his mouth, the words just rolled out like he was making a speech in a big auditorium. ("Preacher's voice," Dad said later. "Comes from years and years of practice.")

Suddenly it was time to say goodbye. Mom and Dad were in the car and waving. It hit me then: I was alone among strangers in a strange place. All I had to remind me of home was a bag of toys. I tried not to cry, but my eyes must have teared up. Then I felt an arm around my shoulder, squeezing me gently.

"A little frightening, isn't it?" Grandfather said. "It must be like the time I got off a plane alone in a strange country. I couldn't even understand the language they spoke."

"What did you do?" I asked.

"First I took a deep breath and swallowed hard. Try it."

I did. It helped a little. "Then what did you do?"

"I told myself that everything was all right. I had come there to work and discover things, and that was what I would do. Then I started to do it."

"Was that the Land of Messy Potatoes?"

"No. The actual name is Mesopotamia. It's from the Greek language and it means The Land Between Two Rivers."

"What two rivers?"

"The Tigris and the Euphrates. The country is now called Iraq. Come into the den. I'll show you where it is on the globe."

The den was another of those small rooms with high ceilings and full of old furniture. There was no carpet, but a collection of rugs covered the floor like a huge patchwork quilt. I remember how everything smelled of wood polish and stale pipe smoke. Books and papers were shelved, stacked and piled everywhere. In one corner stood a large roll-top desk with an ancient typewriter on it. The globe sat in another corner. It was twice as big as a basketball and mounted on a heavy wooden stand so that you could spin it. "Right now we are here," Grandfather said as he placed a hand on the United States. "And the ancient kingdom of Mesopotamia, where I went researching, is clear over here." His hand swept across the Atlantic Ocean, across Europe and down into what I later learned was called the Middle East.

"But where is the land of Messy Potatoes?" I asked.

Grandfather shrugged. "Nobody knows that, not even me. It could be just about anywhere. Does that surprise you?"

"Yes," I said.

"Well, there's a story about why that is so. It's a very long story, and it could take a long time to tell it."

"More than one night?" I asked.

"Many nights. Maybe many weeks. Maybe many years. It depends upon how much you want to hear."

"Can we start tonight?"

"Certainly," he said. "But right now, why don't you un-pack and explore? I put you in the room your mother had when she was your age."

"Was it Uncle Hugh's room too?" I blurted it out before I could stop myself. I still remember the look of sadness that passed across his face like the shadow of a cloud.

"No," he finally said. "That room stays locked. Someday, if you prove yourself, I may let you see it."

I wasn't sure what he meant by that, but I knew I wasn't supposed to ask. I explored all the rooms that were unlocked. They all had furniture, but they also had that empty smell that builds up in rooms when people never go in them.

Mrs. Phelps fixed dinner for us that night. She was short and plump. When she stood next to Grandfather, she reminded me of a bowling ball about to knock over a bowling pin. She sat with us at dinner and kicked me under the table for not bowing my head when Grandfather said grace. I didn't forget again.

That night Grandfather came up to tuck me in. Then he sat on the edge of the bed. He had no book, just a piece of paper with a few scribbles on it.

"You wanted to hear about the King of Messy Potatoes, I believe?" he asked in the way that grownups do when they already know the answer. I nodded, but said nothing.

"Very well. We'll begin. Once upon a time, there was a boy named Spud. . . ."

"Spud?" I almost shouted. "What kind of a name is that?"

"It's the name of the hero of our story."

"But why was he called Spud?"

"If you listen, I will tell you," Grandfather said. He cleared his throat and began again.

Chapter Two

In which Spud loses Ma and two brothers,
misses a story, and finds a remarkable bird
· · · · · · · · · · · · · · · · ·

Once upon a time there was a boy named Spud. He lived with his mother and two older brothers on a small farm way out in the country and miles from any town. Spud's two brothers were called Will and Tom. His mother was called Ma, and she was always kind to him. But Will and Tom could be pretty mean at times.

Spud never knew what Ma's real name was, and he couldn't remember his daddy at all. He had gone off to fight in a war somewhere, back when Spud was just a baby, and he had never come back. Ma told Spud that his daddy didn't want to go be a soldier. But the king and their neighbor, Count Rolph, didn't give him any choice. One morning the count's men handed him a sword and told him to march with them to fight the king's enemies, and that's the last anyone ever saw of Spud's daddy.

Sometimes Spud thought about his daddy when he was weeding the potato patch or hoeing the potato patch or planting the spuds or digging them up. He had lots of time to think down there, because he was always digging, hoeing, planting or weeding the spuds. That's why his lazy older brothers called him Spud.

What was Spud like? Well, he was short, still just a boy. His brother Will took most of the height. And he was kind of thin. His brother Tom took most of the fat. But Spud got most of the brains, because his lazy brothers weren't interested in them. So Spud, along with Ma, did all the thinking for the family.

Spud's favorite thinking place was an old stump right in the center of the messy potato field. It must have been a mighty tree once, but by the time Spud came along, it was just an old stump where he could sit and think when he got tired from working in the field. Then he would close his eyes, which were gray like the gray of the sea before a storm, and think about life or truth or whatever else came into his head.

His face had already lost the roundness of the faces of most boys his age. It was the face of someone growing up very fast.

One afternoon Spud was thinking about what it would be like to have a proper name. His brothers had called him Spud for so long that he was stuck with it. When he asked Ma what his real name was, she said she'd forgotten. This kind of upset Spud. He was proud of the potatoes he grew, but he didn't especially want to be named for them.

People said they were the best-tasting spuds ever grown, but they only grew in one messy little field down behind the cottage Spud's daddy had built many years before Spud was born. Nobody knew why, but Spud thought about it a lot.

One day Spud thought about how ornery kings and counts could be, and how they messed up the lives of ordinary folk. "By gum!" he muttered. "If I was ever a king, I'd treat my subjects nice and not march 'em off to fight in some war they know nothing about!"

Before he could think much more, Ma called him back to the cottage for dinner. They had just started to eat when Spud's brother Will banged on the table and said, "Ma, Tom, Spud! I've been doing me some thinking!"

This surprised Spud. He knew a lot about his older brothers by now, and he knew that thinking was something neither Will nor Tom did very often. In fact, they each did as little thinking as they could.

"What have you been thinking about, Will?" Ma asked as politely as she could. She was a little surprised herself.

"I've been thinking that I'm about all growed up now, and it's time I went out into the world to seek my fortune."

"Oh Will!" Ma said. "Have you been listening to story-tellers?"

"There was one stopped by Count Rolph's castle last week, when I was up there delivering a load of spuds for the count's big banquet," Will admitted. "He told some right exciting tales about brave young lads who slew dragons and rescued princesses and things like that. I'd like to give it a try. It sure sounds like a lot more fun than staying here and working hard all day raising spuds."

That made Spud kind of mad, since Will and Tom never did any real work at all, if they could help it. Sure, they would haul the spuds over to Count Rolph's big castle, just so they could laugh and sing and flirt with the servant girls. But did they ever weed or hoe or dig or plant anything? Nope. Those were Spud's jobs.

"How do you reckon to make your way out there?" Ma asked. "I don't recall hearing of any stray dragons or princesses around these parts."

"I know that," said Will. "That's what I was thinking about. I reckon I'll have to go out and hunt 'em up. So what I'd like to do, right here and now, is claim my rightful inheritance."

"Well," Ma said, "I don't hardly have anything to give you. We've got a horse, a cow, a dog, and a cat. I suppose I could give you the choice of 'em, and that could be your inheritance."

"Hmm!" said Will, and he thought for a bit. Thinking did not come easily for Will. He wrinkled his brow and scratched his head, which Spud wished he wouldn't do during dinner. Will didn't wash very often, and the things that fell from his head onto the table tended to spoil Spud's appetite.

"I reckon the horse would do me the most good," Will finally decided. "If you'll pack me a lunch, I'll saddle him up and be on my way first thing in the morning."

"What are you going to use for a weapon?" asked Spud, who tended to think of things his brothers overlooked. "Daddy didn't leave any sword or lance behind. There's just some old farm tools."

This caused Will to think and scratch some more, and Spud was sorry he brought the matter up. At last Will's eyes brightened and he snapped his fingers. Spud realized that his older brother had an idea, and that was really unusual!

"There's the old pitchfork out in the barn!" Will cried. "We don't use it much, and if I sharpen up the points some, it'd be almost as good as a spear!"

Spud decided not to mention shields, helmets or armor. There was no telling what else Will might decide to carry off, and the family needed everything they had. Of course, Will didn't work very much, and he ate an awful lot. So maybe the loss of a horse, a pitchfork, and an older brother wouldn't be *too* bad.

Early next morning Will saddled the only horse, took the only pitchfork and a knapsack full of food, and rode off to look for adventure. As to what he found and what happened to him. . . we don't know, because this story is not going to be about Will.

Spud continued to work in the field every day, while Tom kind of took over Will's old job. That is, he loafed around, ate an awful lot and once in a while took a load of goods up to Count Rolph's castle. One day he returned with a funny, far-away look in his eye. "Ma Spud!" he said that night at dinner. "I've been doing me some thinking."

Ma and Spud again looked surprised. Tom did even less thinking than Will, if such a thing was possible.

"What have you been thinking about, Tom?" Ma asked.

"I've been thinking that I'm just about all growed up now, and it's time I went out into the world to seek my fortune," Tom said.

"Oh Tom! Have you been listening to storytellers too?"

"Well, there was one up at Count Rolph's place, yesterday, when I took the load of spuds up there for his big party," Tom admitted. "He told some right wonderful tales. So I reckon it's time I got me my rightful inheritance and. . ."

"But Will already took the horse and the pitchfork," Spud said. "So you can't very well be a knight."

"The feller this here storyteller told about weren't no knight," Tom replied. "He was a wandering minstrel and a poet. Reckon you don't need a horse or a spear to do that."

"But you do need to sing songs, recite poetry and play an instrument," said Spud, "and I never heard you do any of that."

"Reckon I could learn," Tom said after scratching his head as he thought about it. Spud shut his eyes. Tom washed even less often than Will, and what fell from his head onto the table Spud did not even want to see. "Singin' 'n playin' 'n recitin' can't be all that hard. I could probably get the hang of it in a day or two. So I'd like to claim my rightful inheritance."

"But Tom," Ma said, "your Daddy didn't leave any musical instruments behind. We've got nothing for you to play."

Tom thought and scratched some more. Spud kept his eyes tightly shut until he heard his brother snap his fingers. "I can take the old washtub and the dipper!" Tom cried. "They'll sound almost like a drum, and *that's* a musical instrument!"

Spud shook his head, but Ma just sighed. "All right then," she said. "You can have them and one of the animals for your rightful inheritance. Do you want the cow, or the dog, or the cat?"

Tom had to think and scratch for several minutes on that one. "Reckon I'll take me the dog," he said at last. "He can kinda sing along with me. Leastwise, he can howl real good."

So, early the next morning, Tom took the dog, the old washtub, and the dipper and set off down the road to seek his fortune. What became of him and whether he ever found it. . . well, we will never know. Because this story is not about Tom either.

Now Spud and Ma were left alone to run the farm as best they could. Ma cried some because she missed her two older sons, but Spud was rather happy they were gone, though he tried not to let it show in front of Ma. They had been working the farm alone for about a week when Ma told Spud that Count

Rolph needed a load of potatoes up at his castle.

"Try not to listen to any storytellers, Son," she warned him. "Remember what happened to your poor, simple brothers."

Spud promised he would be on guard in case anyone tried to tell him a story. Then he set off for Count Rolph's castle. The day was very warm, with no hint of a breeze. A raven flying overhead was the only moving creature he could see.

Spud had never seen the castle before. He had never met Count Rolph nor any of his family. He wasn't even sure where the castle was or what it looked like. But Ma said it was a big stone house, and he wouldn't miss it if he kept right to the road.

Sure enough, he didn't miss it. Count Rolph's castle was the biggest building Spud had ever seen. Actually, it was only average as castles go. But if you have never seen anything bigger than a cottage, then even an average castle looks pretty impressive.

"Wow!" Spud said as he stared at the massive walls. "What sort of person can this count be if he has a house like this?"

He soon decided that Count Rolph was not very nice. He was very large and he smiled too much. Ma had said that people who smiled too much could be worse than people who never smiled at all. His mouth smiles, but his eyes don't, Spud thought as he gazed at the count for the first time.

"Welcome, Young ah. . . Spud, is it?" the count cried in a voice that didn't really mean it.

"That's what everybody calls me, Count," Spud said. "We've kinda forgot what my real name was."

"How quaint!" The count politely sneered. "Why do they call you Spud?"

"'Cause I spend most of my time working in the potato field," Spud replied. The count gave him another false smile.

"Oh yes, the potatoes. Did you bring them?"

"You can bet I did, Count!" said Spud. "Your steward is stowing 'em away right now."

Even as he spoke, Spud was thinking. Why did Count Rolph send word for him to deliver the potatoes? Why not just send one of his own servants to collect them?

"You have done well," said the count. "It will soon be dinner time. You must stay and eat with my kitchen staff. I believe there will be some entertainment."

"A storyteller, maybe?" Spud asked.

"Indeed," smiled the count. "I have heard he tells wondrous tales about faraway lands and daring young lads who venture off to seek their fortunes there. You should find it most interesting."

Spud remembered Ma's warning and had no wish to stay and listen.

But the count was a count, after all. And if a count asks a peasant to stay for a while, the peasant would do well to agree. Spud knew little about counts and their ways, but he was no fool either. He stayed.

Dinner in the kitchen with the staff was not as fancy as the count's big banquet table, but it was still bigger and better than anything Spud had ever had. He ate until he was comfortably full. Then he waited to see what would happen next.

A long, lean man with a face as sharp as a knife pushed his chair back from the table, reached down and picked up a curious instrument. It looked something like a small harp. He brushed the strings carelessly a few times, turned a couple of pegs and then began to pick out a tune.

"I'll tell you a story of long, long ago," he said as he played. The servants all bent forward to listen, but something else caught Spud's eye. Just behind the storyteller, perched on the ledge of an open window, was a raven. He remembered seeing a raven on his way to the castle. Was it the same bird? Why was it there?

The raven seemed to be listening and nodding as though it understood the story. Spud got so interested in the bird and its antics that he ignored the storyteller. None of the servants noticed the bird, but Spud sensed the raven was trying to tell him something. But what was it?

Suddenly the raven flapped its wings once, then flew away. At the same time, Spud heard the storyteller say, "And so ends my tale." All the count's servants clapped noisily and Spud, not wanting to be rude, did the same. The storyteller gave him a curious smile and then left the table.

"Well, Young Man," the count said as Spud prepared to leave. "Did you like the entertainment?"

"It was all right, Count," Spud replied.

"Only all right?" The count seemed disappointed. "I thought he could do better than that. I shall make him try harder next time." Again the count's mouth smiled, but his eyes did not.

On his way home Spud saw the raven again. The bird would fly on ahead of him, perch in a tree, wait for him to pass and then fly on again. It was very curious and un-bird-like behavior, and it topped off a very curious and unlikely day.

Why would the count invite a lowly delivery boy to stay to dinner? Why would he have the entertainment in the kitchen for the servants and not out in the main hall for his family and guests? Why would a raven stop in to listen? And why was it following him? In fact, why would the count be buying potatoes from Ma and him in the first place? Surely he had land enough to grow his own.

It was enough to put Spud in a botheration.

Ma was waiting with a worried look. "Did you listen to any storytellers?" she asked.

"Naw," said Spud. "There was one, but I paid no mind. You see, this here raven perched on a ledge behind him and. . ."

"Good!" Ma said, and things went back to normal for a week or so. Then Count Rolph sent word that he needed another load of potatoes. Spud filled the cart, harnessed Blossom the cow, and set off once more for the castle.

"Remember, Son!" Ma warned as he started down the road. "Don't you go listening to any storytellers!"

Once more the day was warm and windless, and once more Spud saw a raven flying overhead. Again the count welcomed him and invited him to dinner in the kitchen with his staff. The same storyteller was there, but so was the raven on the window ledge behind him. And again Spud got so interested in the bird that he paid no attention to the story.

"How did you like the story this time?" asked the count as Spud prepared to leave. Again his mouth smiled, but his eyes did not.

"It was pretty fair," Spud said.

A flash of anger shot across the count's face before he could smile again. Spud didn't notice this. Out of the corner of one eye he had caught just a glimpse of a beautiful girl as she left the banquet hall by another door. It happened so quickly that he couldn't remember later what she looked like. But he was ready to swear that she was the most beautiful girl he had ever seen. Of course, he hadn't seen very many, living out where he did.

And once again the raven followed him all the way home.

A week later the count sent Ma and Spud a third order for potatoes. Spud filled the cart and harnessed the cow, but Ma sent him back to the field and took the reins herself.

"Third time means trouble," she said. "Reckon it's best for you to stay here and let me take care of it."

As she started, Spud saw the raven flying above her. That made him feel a little easier, but he was still in a botheration. What trouble did she mean? He wanted to follow her, but she had told him to stay. Spud had always done what Ma told him to do.

Well. . . almost always.

Soon, the sun had dropped low in the afternoon sky, and Ma had not come back. Orders or no orders, Spud set out to find her.

The afternoon was heavy with heat and silence. Again, nothing seemed to move except himself. He searched the sky for the raven, but he didn't see it. Then, suddenly, he heard it.

"Quark!" came a call from a thicket at the side of the road. It was a cry of defiance and despair. "Quark!" Spud knew it was also a call for help. He plunged into the thicket and found the bird. The raven was on the ground with its back against a tree. A broken wing drooped uselessly at its side. A small fox crouched just beyond the reach of its powerful beak. It knew it had the bird trapped and was waiting for an opportunity to pounce.

Spud yelled, grabbed up a stick, and charged. The fox slunk away into the thicket. This is curious, Spud thought. I go looking for Ma and end up rescuing a bird. He held the stick down by the raven's feet, and the bird hopped onto it.

"Are you the bird that followed me and Ma to the castle?" he wondered. The bird nodded as if it understood him.

"Well, I can't leave you here, and I can't take you with me neither. So what am I gonna do with you?"

As if in answer, the bird hopped from the stick onto Spud's arm. "I think you know something," Spud said. "I just wish you could talk." As soon as he said that, the raven jabbed him in the arm with its beak.

"Owww!" yelled Spud. "What did you do that for, you ungrateful bird!"

"I'm sorry," the raven answered, "but you did want me to talk."

Chapter Three

In which Spud learns new things about his
family and plows a furrow right through a stream
· · · · · · · · · · · · · · · · ·

"You can speak!" Spud cried.

"Of course," the raven said. "You asked me to, after all."

"But how?"

"One drop of your blood in my throat and I can speak your language all day," the raven replied. "But since you only speak one language, my ability is limited right now. Last year, I nipped a very learned monk and became the instant master of six languages and three regional dialects."

The raven hopped from Spud's arm to his shoulder, cocked its head to one side and asked, "What do you want to talk about?"

"What happened to Ma?" Spud demanded.

"They took her," the raven said.

"Count Rolph and his servants? Why would they do that? We ain't anybody special or important."

"Ah, but you are!" said the raven. "You own a piece of land that may be the most valuable earth in the kingdom. In several kingdoms. Perhaps the most valuable piece of land on earth! What do you say to that?"

"I'd say that was crazy!" Spud exclaimed as the raven tried to hop from his shoulder to the top of his head, missed, and tumbled to the ground. "All we own is that cottage, a couple of sheds and the messy old field of potatoes," he added as he picked the raven up and set it back on his arm.

The raven shook its head and snapped its beak. "Wrong! Very wrong! Three springs flow beneath that field: The Spring of Health, the Spring of Knowledge, and the Spring of Power. Dig right at the base of that old stump and you will strike any or all of them. Drink from them and you will have power, the wisdom to use it properly, and a long, healthy life. What is more valuable than that?"

"So that's why our potatoes taste so good," Spud said. "But how did we come to own the field? And why did I never hear of it? And how did Count Rolph come to find out? And why did he take Ma? And what can I do about it?"

"You can begin by asking one question at a time," the raven said as it ruffled its neck feathers. "You have it because your grandfather saved the life of the king's father in battle. The king's father gave him the land as a reward, and he had it written into law that the land would remain in your family for as long as any of your grandfather's sons and their descendants were there to live on it. Thus the count cannot seize it or buy it."

"Why was I never told about this?" Spud asked.

"Because each father can only tell one son, and that son must choose to live on the land," said the raven. "Your father was the son chosen by his father, but you were just a baby when he was taken off to fight. I'm sure he was waiting to choose you, since both your brothers fell somewhat short of being the smartest lads in the world."

"Ma must have known something," Spud said. "She tried to warn me, and she went in my place to protect me."

"She knew the land was special, but she didn't know why. Your father could not tell her outright, but he dropped enough hints for her to get an idea. Your mother was very smart. Your brothers, alas, were not. Next question."

"How did Count Rolph find out about it?"

"The count is not a very good man," the raven said. "Nor is the present king. They are both more weak than wicked, but they don't have any standards they believe in. When morally weak people acquire power, they can cause more mischief than the truly evil. And when there is a chance to cause trouble, there are forces, some call them spirits, who will gladly do it."

"So one of these, uh, spirits told the count?"

The raven nodded. "A tempter. A very minor one, since the count was not enough of a man to require anything stronger. The count learned that he could not have your land as long as one of you boys lived on it. But it would all be his if you all left it of your own free will."

"So that was why he had the storyteller at his castle?"

"Indeed," the raven answered. "He stopped up the ears of his own servants with wax, so they could not hear the tales. But he ordered them to pretend they were listening so that you and your brothers would not get suspicious."

"Did Ma listen to the storyteller too?" Spud asked. He couldn't picture his mother being seized by the desire to go off hunting for adventures. Will and Tom were dumb enough. But not Ma!

"No," said the raven. "They were expecting you. It was no use to tempt her with stories, so they simply took her."

"But where?"

The raven bowed its head in shame. "That, alas, I cannot tell you. You see, I made a very bad mistake," it confessed. "It was such a small, minor tempter that I thought I could overcome it all by myself. So I flew down and challenged it."

The bird looked ruefully at its injured wing. "It crippled me with one stroke and left me as food for the foxes. I'm very lucky you came along when you did. But now I'm powerless and stuck in this form."

"You mean you're not really a raven?" Spud asked.

"Only when I choose to be," the bird answered. "It's a nice shape for moving about the world. But I'm not a real raven. . . just like that tempter was not a real storyteller."

"Then why don't you change to another form?" Spud asked. "A bird with a broken wing ain't much use to anyone."

The raven shook its head and clacked its beak sadly. "A spirit like mine cannot leave an injured body until the body heals or dies, and mine won't heal until that tempter is destroyed."

"You mean I should have let the fox kill you?" Spud asked.

"Of course not! How can I help you if I'm dead? And you are going to need my help before the sun comes up tomorrow, my young friend!"

"But. . ."

"No time for talking!" the raven urged. "We must get back to your cottage as quickly as we can. The count expects you to come looking for your mother. When he realizes you aren't coming to him, he's going to go after you."

Spud set the raven on his shoulder and started for the cottage at a run. Then he stopped. The bird seemed to be overlooking one very important point. "But why are we going back to the cottage?" he asked. "Won't that be the first place Count Rolph will look?"

"The count doesn't like to go out at night. He won't come for you until morning. That will give us time to escape."

"I don't see what good that will do," Spud said as he set off at a walk. "If we leave, he takes the land. If we stay, he takes the land and us. We lose either way."

"But suppose we were to leave *and* take the land with us," the raven suggested.

"Huh?" Spud cried. "How do we do that?"

"Get me back to your cottage and I'll show you," the raven said. It was dark by the time they reached the cottage, but Spud knew that a full moon would soon rise. The skies were cloudless, so there would be plenty of light for traveling. But where were they going? What was the raven's plan? And who was this bird anyway?

"Do you have a plow and harness?" the raven asked.

"Of course we do," Spud said. "But what do we want with it? Count Rolph is going to seize the land, remember? Do you want me to plow it for him before we go?"

"No," the raven said. "We are going to save it, and ourselves as well. Harness up the cow and be ready to do what I tell you. We don't have time to stand here and argue. The count won't wait long after sunrise."

Spud could move quickly when he had to. He roused the cow and soon had it harnessed to the plow. "Now what?" he asked.

"Lead it over to the old stump in the field and bring a spade with you," the bird replied.

I'm in the biggest mess in my life, Spud thought as he hunted for the spade. And who do I have for a helper? A crippled, talking, totally crazy bird!

Spud expected trouble with the cow as well. The animal believed that days were for work and nights for sleep and got very cross if she was roused from her rest. But for once she seemed willing, almost eager to help.

"A fine beast, indeed!" the raven said. "What do you call her?"

"Will and Tom just called her the cow," Spud replied. "But I named her Blossom because she likes to eat flowers in the spring and summer."

"A fine name for a fine cow," the raven agreed. "All creatures need a name. You have no dignity without one."

"What's yours, then?" Spud asked.

"In my present form I have none," the raven answered sadly. "I cannot use my former name, because it goes with my former form. And no one has seen fit to name me as a raven."

"Then I'll give you a name," Spud decided. "Hmm, I can't call you John or Jeanette, since I don't know if you're a boy or a girl raven. Which are you, by the way?"

"It's been a long time since I was a boy," the raven answered, "but I was one once. Please, though, I beg you. Don't give me a common name like George or Herman or Jean Paul."

"I will call you Brokenwing," Spud decided. "That seems to describe you pretty well right now. I'll bandage up that wing too, as soon as we finish whatever you're so all-fired eager to do."

"Since you saved me and named me, I'm now your servant," said Brokenwing. "I won't give you orders, but I will give advice, and I hope you will take it more often than not."

"Don't seem to have much choice," said Spud. "Tell me what I'm supposed to do with this here plow and spade."

"My advice is to take the spade and dig a hole at the base of the stump. When you strike water, dig again where I show you. Then you'll dig a third hole and perhaps a fourth."

Spud marched out to the messy field and jabbed his spade into the soft earth at the base of the old stump. How did this all happen? he wondered silently. I set out to find Ma and ended up rescuing a talking raven that wants my blood, and here I am digging up a tree stump. Then I'm gonna plow a field that someone is going to take away from me tomorrow morning. . . but somehow I'm going to escape and take the field with me. If this ain't a botheration, then I don't know what is!

Spud had dug perhaps a foot when water began oozing into the hole. "Deep enough," said the raven. "Now, if you will dig here and here, you will complete the first part of your task." He stabbed the soft earth with his beak to indicate the spots.

This puzzled Spud. It was high summer, just past the solstice, and he should have to dig several feet to strike water. Furthermore, the old stump was on high ground in the middle of the field. Must be the springs, he decided as he dug.

"Now what?" Spud asked as the water oozed into the third hole.

"My advice, Dear Master," said Brokenwing, "is to scoop up mud from all three holes, mix it well and smear it over the point of your plow." Spud shrugged and did as the raven advised.

"Now you are ready to plow," Brokenwing said.

"But this field has already been plowed!" Spud protested. "I did it myself more than two months ago. If I plow it again, I'll ruin the crop!"

"You are not going to plow the field," the raven answered. "You are going to set the boundaries of your kingdom."

"My kingdom?" Spud exclaimed. "I'm not a king! I'm not even a count! I'm just a plain old peasant!"

"You will be a king if you follow my advice," Brokenwing replied. "But you will have to hurry. Are you good with a plow?"

"Been doing it for years," Spud said. "Will and Tom never liked to work that hard. They made it my job as soon as I was big enough to handle it."

"Good!" said the raven. "Then start right at the base of the stump and make a single furrow. The moon is just rising and will give you light enough to see, but you must finish before midnight!"

"Where do I go?" Spud asked.

"Wherever you wish," the raven said. "But you must make a complete loop and reach the starting point before midnight. If you can do that, everything within the loop will be yours!"

Spud had no idea how that could happen, but he shoved the point of the plow into the ground and gently shook the reins. "Ho, Blossom!" he said softly and made a clicking sound with his teeth. It was a signal Blossom knew well. She leaned into the harness and the plow began to move.

It was an old wooden plow that Spud's granddaddy had made from the tree that was now the old stump. Lightning had struck the tree and killed it when Spud's daddy was just a boy. Granddaddy had sheathed the plow point with iron and used the rest of the tree to build the cottage. Now all that was left of the tree was a stump, but the cottage still stood and the plow still worked.

In fact, it had never plowed better. The point cut through the hard earth like a sharp knife through soft cheese. Spud had to look behind to be sure he was cutting a furrow. He saw the dark line rolling out behind him like a ribbon in the moonlight.

Brokenwing hopped on the frame of the plow and carefully made his way up the handle, onto Spud's arm and then up to his shoulder. There he perched and watched as Spud guided Blossom across the land. When Spud began to turn around the field, the raven clacked his beak.

"Why turn here?" he asked.

"Because this is the border of our land."

"Who says so?"

"Well, Count Rolph, I guess."

"The count plans to seize your land. Do you think he will use it for good?"

"Reckon he won't," said Spud. "He sure don't take very good care of his own."

"Then consider taking some of it for yourself," the raven urged. "You can be master of whatever you can encircle with a furrow before midnight."

I think this bird's pod is short a few peas, Spud thought. Yes, he could run a furrow around a great deal of land in a couple of hours, but how could he claim it and hold it? He was alone. Count Rolph had dozens of servants and guards, and the count was a friend of the king, who had an army. Something inside, however, urged him to trust Brokenwing's word. He swung the plow away from the border of the messy potato field and began to cut a furrow across the countryside.

"Don't go widdershins," the raven warned. "Make all your turns to the right."

The plow continued to cut through the earth with almost no resistance. Spud had never had an easier time of it. He had never worked by moonlight either. His days had always been so hard that he had fallen asleep right after supper, only to wake with the dawn and begin the cycle of work all over again. Plowing by night was a strange and thrilling new experience.

He cut the furrow well away from the cottage, around a hill and then, heading west, across the road that led to Count Rolph's castle. The plow point sliced through the road as easily as it had across the field. Blossom moved at a steady walk and seemed to be enjoying herself. It was the easiest furrow he had ever cut.

Spud counted the paces in his head. One hundred, then two hundred. He started to turn Blossom to the right, then decided against it. If this was just a game, then why not play it for all it was worth? He took another two hundred paces, then two hundred more. The plow now sliced through part of

Count Rolph's estate. Spud smiled at the thought and turned Blossom toward the castle.

They came to a small stream. Spud thought, why not? He flicked the reins to signal Blossom to wade in. The cow seemed to enjoy the game too. She waded right across the stream, dragging the plow behind her. Spud had to push down hard when the water reached up to his chest, but he managed to keep the furrow unbroken.

"Good work!" Brokenwing said. "Most plowmen would have turned aside at the bank. Just remember you must cross the stream again on your way back."

Spud was now beginning to believe that he really could control the land inside the furrow, though he still didn't understand how he would do it. He continued toward the castle, taking in two more unused fields and an abandoned cottage as he went. A wild thought struck him. Should he take in the castle itself?

No, he decided. He did not like having Count Rolph as a master, so he probably wouldn't like having him for a subject either. Besides, he wasn't likely to have enough time to cut all the way around the castle and then get back.

Time! The thought made him turn east across another field. He crossed the road again, then plowed his way into the clump of trees and bushes where he had rescued Brokenwing earlier in the day. Moving to the right around the trees cost him some territory.

After he had passed through the trees and onto open ground, Spud thought of the stream. He would have to cross it again going south. Where was it shallow and where was it deep?

Brokenwing shifted uneasily on his shoulder. "I suggest we turn south right away," he warned. "Time is not going to wait for us!"

Spud turned Blossom to the right once again and cut a straight line for the stream. It was narrower here, but probably deeper, and the banks were steep. Could they get down? Could they make it back up? And what would he do if the water was over his head?

Brokenwing seemed to share his thoughts. The raven hopped from his shoulder to the top of his head and clacked its beak nervously. "I'm afraid this is going to be difficult," it warned. "Are you good at holding your breath?"

"Hang on!" Spud cried. "We're gonna find out right now!"

He flicked the reins, clicked his tongue, and Blossom stumbled and slid down the bank and into the stream. Spud followed, pushing down hard on the plow to keep the point in the earth.

This is no longer funny, he thought. Why am I doing it?

Blossom had to swim before she reached midstream, and the mostly wooden plow wanted to float free. It took all of Spud's strength to keep it in the stream bed. When the water reached his chin, he took the deepest breath he could, ducked under and pushed with all his might. His feet slipped and scrabbled on the bottom, and his lungs felt like they were on fire. Then he felt Blossom climbing, and a moment later his head broke the surface again.

Climbing the opposite bank was harder than going down. Twice Blossom lost her footing and almost tumbled back on him. Then she reached the top and dragged Spud and the plow up after her.

Safe! But where was Brokenwing?

Then he felt pains in his scalp and knew the raven was still up there with its claws dug in. "Hey! Relax! Turn loose! We made it!" Spud said.

"I suggest we postpone the celebration," Brokenwing replied as he hopped back down to Spud's shoulder. "We still have ground to cover and not much time to do it!"

Spud flicked the reins again. Blossom sensed the urgency and broke into an awkward trot. Fortunately, the land beyond the stream was flat. Spud looked for landmarks. Where was his cottage? Where was the field? Where was the stump? There they were! Up ahead and to the right!

"This is going to be very close!" Brokenwing warned.

Spud turned Blossom west again and aimed for the field. As he reached the southeast corner, he could see the dark line of the furrow up ahead. He urged Blossom to a last burst of speed, and the plow sliced across the furrow. His track looked more like a blob than a circle or square, but it was complete.

"Quickly!" Brokenwing urged. "Pull it from the ground and head for the stump!" This was more command than advice, but Spud obeyed.

"Now what?" he asked when they reached the stump.

Before Brokenwing could answer, a terrible tremor shook the earth and a terrific blast of wind knocked Spud off his feet and slammed him against the stump. His head struck the hard oak and the sky seemed to explode into millions of brilliant lights.

Chapter Four

In which Spud gets a headache, a title, a strange
new weapon, and the job of chief cook for his subjects
· · · · · · · · · · · · · · · · ·

Day had broken by the time Spud awoke and found himself lying next to the stump. His head felt like it had broken, too. Very carefully, with the tip of a finger, he touched the throbbing lump just above and behind his right ear.

"Ouch!"

Spud shut his eyes against the pain and waited for the throbbing to go away. When he felt a little better, he opened them again and carefully looked around. He felt dizzy and quickly shut them once more. The land seemed to bob gently up and down. . .

Spud waited until the ache was endurable, then tried again. He wasn't dizzy. The land really *was* moving gently up and down, yes, up and down. Something else was also wrong.

The sun should have been in the east, if it was morning, or way over in the west, if it was late afternoon. So what was it doing on the *northern* horizon? It was either coming up or going down right over the road that led to Count Rolph's castle. Spud had never before seen the sun there.

He got to his feet and sat on the stump. Had this all been a dream? No, there was Blossom, still harnessed to the plow and grazing nearby. He could see the furrow leading away from the stump to where it disappeared into fog at the edge of the field. Why was there fog at this time of year? And which direction was which? It was all very confusing, And with his head pounding like six blacksmiths hammering horseshoes inside, Spud didn't feel much like figuring answers.

Bit by bit, the pieces of yesterday's adventures came back to him. He recalled the race with the plow, talking raven. . .

Brokenwing! He could explain things! Where was he?

"Quark!" the raven called from behind the stump.

"There you are!" Spud cried. "What's happened here?"

"Quark!" the raven replied.

Then Spud remembered what he had to do. "Why not?" he muttered as he stuck out an arm. "I can't feel much worse. Ouch!"

"Sorry, Your Majesty," Brokenwing said. "But it's a small price for an entire day of conversation, companionship and absolutely sound advice."

"Easy to say when you're not the one being stuck!" grumbled Spud. "But tell me this, you bloodthirsty bird. Where are we and why is everything all turned around?"

"Where are we?" Brokenwing repeated as he preened his feathers. "I have no idea. We are adrift, Your Majesty. Adrift in both time and space, so I don't know *where* we are or *when* we are. I can only tell you that we are definitely *not* where we were last night."

"You mean we're. . .floating?" Spud asked. The gentle up-and-down motion of the countryside began to make sense. "On. . .the sea?"

"The wine dark sea, as Homer put it," the raven agreed. "The sea of time as well as space, where anything and everything is possible. Ah, Your Majesty! Perhaps I could serve you as tutor, now that you have your own kingdom. I could teach you the classics or applied mathematics or. . ."

"What do you mean. . .my own kingdom? And why do you keep calling me Your Majesty? I ain't no king! What happened to Count Rolph and the land where I lived?"

"The count now owns a rather large and very deep lake on the site where your new kingdom once stood, Your Majesty. What he will do with it. . . I don't know. Perhaps he will learn how to fish."

"Don't call me Your Majesty! I ain't majestic!"

"But you are!" said Brokenwing. "Then how about Your Highness?"

"I ain't very high neither."

"Your Grace? Your Excellency? Your Lordship?"

"No! No! and No! I ain't none of them things! I'm just plain Spud!"

"Then how about Your Spudship?" Brokenwing offered. "A king must have some kind of title!"

"All right," Spud shrugged. "Call me that if you want. But what happened to Ma? And how are we gonna find her?"

"The tempter took her somewhere or transformed her or maybe both," said Brokenwing. "The only way we can find her is to find him."

"How do we do that?" Spud asked.

"We don't have to. He'll find us. You don't have to look for temptation. It comes looking for you. The trick is to recognize and overcome it, and that's not easy."

Spud did not understand all that Brokenwing told him, but he was curious about his new kingdom and where it might be going. He unharnessed Blossom, set the raven on his shoulder and began to follow the furrow he had plowed the night before. Blossom, eager for company, tagged along behind them.

The sky overhead was clear, but a bank of fog seemed to encircle Spud's island. The closer he got to the edge of his land, the thicker it became. At the very rim where the furrow turned, Spud could hear the ocean lapping just below the track. But the fog was too thick to see anything.

"Don't worry," said Brokenwing. "It will clear off when we strike land. But now it keeps others from seeing us, and who knows what may be out there? I could tell you tales of pirates. . ."

"I get the idea," Spud said quickly. He turned and headed, well, it would have been north the day before; now it was either east or west, and that was changing too. The island appeared to rotate very slowly as it bobbed gently up and down in the sea. I sure hope nothing important falls off, Spud thought as he walked.

A thousand strides brought him back to the fog, so he turned right again. A few hundred more strides and they came to the road and the clump of trees where Spud had rescued Brokenwing from the fox. "I wonder if we still have that critter or did he get left with Count Rolph?" Spud said.

"Time will tell," Brokenwing answered as they walked on in a direction that once was east. "But we should give a thought to whom or what might be in the next land we bump into. You are indeed a king, but you command only a bird and a cow."

"And an old tomcat, if he wasn't prowling out beyond the furrow when I cut it," Spud added. "I haven't seen him today, but that don't mean nothing. He wouldn't be much good in a fight, 'cept with another cat. Far as that goes, none of us are fighters. So what happens if we run up against a king with an army?"

"Two suggestions," Brokenwing replied. "First, believe in yourself. No one else will if you don't. Second, use your brain. The cow is stronger than you are, and the cat is quicker. You know how to think, and that's what makes you their master."

"Okay," said Spud as they walked along. "I guess I'm stuck with being a king. But I sure don't feel like one and I sure don't look like one. All the kings in the stories Ma told me had golden crowns and fancy shields and magical weapons and faithful steeds. Where am I gonna find that stuff around here?"

"Lesson number one: use what's available," Brokenwing replied. "All you really need is here, if you have the wits to see it."

They came to the stream, and Spud hunted for a shallow place to cross. He found one, paused in midstream to taste the water, then made a face and spat it out.

"Salt!" he cried. "The sea is running through it!"

"What did you expect?" asked Brokenwing. "It will run fresh again when we strike another land mass. Meanwhile, the springs by the old stump will provide all the water you need."

"The springs!" Spud murmured. " They seem to have magical powers. I can use them to make what I need. That must be what the bird means."

Spud ran back to the cottage. Stored in the cow shed beside it were the few simple tools the family kept to do their chores. Will had taken the pitchfork, but the saw was still there.

He grabbed the saw and ran back to the stump. Brokenwing had to dig in his claws to keep his perch. If Spud could cut an inch-thick disc from the stump and somehow fasten handles to it, that would serve him as a shield. The saw was heavy, though, and the stump big. Could he do it by himself? He would have to try.

He remembered the mud and how easily the plow had turned the earth when he smeared some on the point. He dug again, coated the saw, and then hefted it into place. It seemed to have less than half its former weight. He set the blade against the stump an inch below the top, took a deep breath and pushed.

Zzzt! The cut went several inches into the stump at one stroke, even though the wood was old, hard oak. He drew the blade back and pushed again. Zzzt! It was almost like cutting through air. Five strokes and he was finished.

Spud fumbled in a pouch he carried on his belt and drew out a small knife. He smeared the blade and cut two small chunks from the stump. Even without the mud, Spud was a good whittler. He soon had carved two handles, one to hold his forearm and another to grip with his hand.

"Now, how do I fasten them?" he thought aloud. "I don't think we have any nails, wait. . . yes, Pegs!"

He whittled four pegs from the stump, smeared them well, then bored holes with his knife point in the handles and the shield and fitted them together with the pegs.

"Good!" said Brokenwing. "When they dry, they will hold tighter than any nail. And if you smear the rest of the shield, it will become very light, but so hard that the strongest sword or ax cannot crack it."

"It's a real nice shield," Spud agreed, "but I don't have any sword to go with it."

"Why do you want a sword?" Brokenwing asked.

"Well, all the kings and knights and squires in the stories Ma told me and my brothers had 'em," Spud replied.

"But what is a sword designed to do?"

Spud thought for a moment, then said, "Destroy whatever you hit with it, I reckon."

"So do you want to be known as a king or as a killer of men?"

"Can you be one without being the other?" Spud asked.

"You'll have to decide that for yourself," Brokenwing told him. "But you will have to sleep every night. What do you want to see in your dreams?"

Spud considered. He was kind by nature, and the thought of bloodshed didn't much appeal to him. "I'd give up the sword if I had something that would protect me without killing," he said.

"Then dig at the base of the stump, just here." The raven jabbed the soft earth with his beak to indicate the spot.

Spud grabbed the spade and went to work. The earth felt very soft and light. What was down there? An arms cache? Buried treasure? The spade struck something hard.

"It's a root!" he exclaimed. "Just a tough old root. What good is that?"

"It's the very toughest part of a very tough old tree, and it's been soaking in the magical springs for years and years," said Brokenwing. "Why don't you dig out a length and cut it free?"

Spud soon had a piece, cut from the main root, the length of his arm and just a bit thicker. He trimmed it, cut a grip for his hand and tried a practice swing.

"Not a bad club," he admitted.

"It's more than just a club," Brokenwing said. "It is *the* club. You, Your Spudship, now wield a nobbeltynook!"

"Never heard of such a thing," Spud remarked.

"Of course you haven't," Brokenwing told him. "There has never been one until now."

"Looks like just a club to me," Spud said as he tested the balance and trimmed it a little more. "What all does it do?"

"One good whack will drive the evil from a person as quickly as a blow from a regular cudgel will scatter his senses," Brokenwing replied. "Stupidity, though, requires two or three whacks, because men are evil by choice, but stupid by nature."

"Then with this. . . what did you call it?"

"Nobbeltynook," Brokenwing pronounced carefully.

". . . this nobbeltynook, I can overcome bad guys without having to kill them. Great idea. . . but will it really work?"

"Yes. But you must never strike in anger, only to protect yourself or those you love."

"Gonna be kinda hard to whack someone without being mad, won't it?" Spud wondered.

"Hard, but not impossible," said the raven, "or maybe it's impossible, but not hard. That's another question you must answer for yourself."

Spud tried to think, but the only thought that came to him was that he had gone a full day with nothing to eat and was terribly, terribly hungry. Ma had always done the cooking. Spud had watched her enough that he figured he could handle the job. Just what was he going to fix?

A couple of spuds from the messy old field. . . that would do for a start. There might be some greens left in Ma's garden, and Ma had made bread just two days ago. Some meat would be nice. Poor peasants only got that on very special feast days.

What about his subjects? Blossom could graze, and Old Tom—if he was still around—could hunt for himself. Brokenwing was helpless, though. What did ravens like? Well, at least with this raven, he could ask.

"Are you hungry?" Spud asked the bird as he bound up broken wing with strips of old cloth. "I was thinking about fixing us some dinner."

"*Thinking* about fixing dinner, or anything else, means nothing, Your Spudship. I suggest we actually *do* it."

"Okay then. What do you like?"

"I'm partial to fish, when I can get it," the raven said.

"I've never had fish before," Spud confessed. "We are. . . I mean, we *were*. . . so far from the sea, and Count Rolph never let anyone fish the streams on his land. Will tried it once, and the count had him whipped for it."

"Let's go down to the rim of your realm," Brokenwing suggested. "Maybe we'll find something there."

"We'll find the fog. I know that," Spud replied without much enthusiasm. He set the raven on his shoulder and hiked along the furrow to the shore.

"Fish! I smell fish!" Brokenwing cried.

"Where?" Spud asked. "The fog's so dang thick I can't see anything!"

"Get down on your hands and knees and feel along the ground just there. . . no. . . a little more to the left. There! Do you feel them?"

"Fish! Two of them, lying right by the furrow!" Spud exclaimed as he stood up with a fish in each hand. "But how did they wind up on the land?"

"They are flying fish, Your Spudship. They probably leaped out of the water to escape some larger fish chasing them, landed in your kingdom and couldn't get back. Providence, indeed. Let's eat!"

Spud took the fish and some potatoes back to the cottage, kindled a fire, and began cooking dinner. The smell of frying flying fish filled the cottage and then drifted outside. Not long after, Spud felt something rub against his leg and heard a voice he'd heard many times.

"Meow!"

Spud smiled. "Hah, Old Tom! You decided to stick around after all? How about some fish heads?"

"Meooow!" the cat agreed.

Brokenwing did not look happy. "If I had two good wings and could fly, Your Spudship, I would not care two pins for that cat or what he thinks when he looks at me. Being the way I am, he might get ideas once the fish are gone. I need to have a talk with him. Would you please pick him up and hold him for a moment?"

Spud picked up the cat and cradled him in his arms, holding his forepaws securely. Brokenwing approached cautiously, then suddenly jabbed Old Tom just behind the ear.

"Meeeooooww!" the cat screeched in protest.

"Meeeooooww!" Brokenwing replied in exactly the same tone. The cat hissed at the raven. The raven hissed back.

It was an interesting discussion, even though Spud couldn't understand it. At last Brokenwing nodded his head, clacked his beak and said, "I think he now understands our respective ranks and what will happen if he gets out of line. Let him go and let's eat."

It was a very curious dinner. Spud sat at the table with the cat on one side of him and the raven on the other. Outside, Blossom's bell tinkled softly as she grazed. Brokenwing pushed part of his fish over to the cat as a peace offering, but Old Tom hissed and stalked out of the cottage.

"He's never going to like me," the raven observed. "I don't think he cares much for you either."

"I'm not surprised," said Spud. He and the cat had never been close. Old Tom was fat and lazy and reminded Spud too much of his brothers.

After dinner they hiked along the furrow again. Brokenwing looked at the fog and ruffled the feathers on his good wing. "It's thinning, Your Spudship," he said. "That means we're going to strike land very soon. We'd best get ready!"

Chapter Five

In which I learn about Hugh's favorite book, a difference between seminary and cemetery, and an attack on a warship
. . . .

My first visit with Grandfather Kneale lasted just three days. He would only tell me about Spud after I was tucked in for the night. I guess he figured it was a good way to get me to go to bed on time.

Other things happened. Jason Mitchell, Mrs. Phelps' grandson, came over on the second day. He was just my age and size. We played outdoors in the backyard and upstairs in some empty rooms, and we only got into one fight.

Jason's grandmother was a great cook. We would sit and watch her fix dinner. Sometimes she would have all four burners and the oven going at once. Pots would boil. Others would simmer. Pans of stuff would bake. From all the activity, you'd think she was cooking for a small army. But there was only the four of us.

She never used a microwave. "Don't trust 'em!" she said when I asked her why. "Neither does your grandfather. Why, I might open the door at the wrong time and those rays could zap right out and cook me on the spot! And what would you do if your cook got cooked? Why, you'd probably starve!"

I was pretty sure the microwaves couldn't get out of the oven. But even if they could, she might not be an easy target. I said she was plump, but "solid" might have been a better word. She didn't jiggle when she moved, like a lot of fat people do, and she could move fast if she wanted.

She proved it one day when Jason and I tried to steal two cookies from a pan that had just come out of the oven. She smacked both our hands, just once and not hard, whisked the pan out of reach and went back to stirring without missing a beat. "Wait till they're cool and then ask!" she said as we retreated.

I think her ambition was to fatten Grandfather up, though she never succeeded. He dished up his own plate and, though he always ate everything he took, he never took much, nor went back for seconds. "Give it to the boys," he said when she urged him to take more. "They're growing and they need it. If I start putting on weight, I'll just have to buy new clothes."

Something in the way he said it made me feel that he didn't like the idea of new clothes. In fact, I don't think he liked anything new, except maybe me. He got me the TV, but would never look at it. "Why won't you watch it?" I asked him once.

"Why should I?" he said. "I get all my news from the paper and all my entertainment from these." He pointed to bookshelves that ran from floor to ceiling in his den. "And there's thousands more in the library if I run out," he added.

"Your grandfather's kinda weird," Jason said on the third day, which led to our only fight. "I mean, he's not *weird* weird," he explained after we had thumped each other and rolled across the backyard and up against the fence. "He's more like a n*ice* weird."

"What do you mean?" I asked as I tried to catch my breath before going at him again.

"It's like he comes from another time," Jason said. "It's like he should have been living a hundred years ago. Or maybe even a thousand years ago."

I didn't like it, but Jason made sense. Grandfather *was* weird, in a nice way. He never watched the tube with me, but he read to me whenever I asked. I remember one book we read that first summer: *The Little Prince*.

We hadn't finished it when Mom came to take me back home, and, while she loaded the suitcase and the toys, Grandfather handed me the book. "Take it with you," he said. "Your mother or father can finish it with you. In a year or so you can read it for yourself. Good books should be read more than once."

"I think it's a good book," I agreed.

"The man who wrote it was very brave. He was a pilot in World War II, even though he was supposed to be too old to fly. And he flew unarmed. His plane had cameras to photograph enemy positions and carried no guns."

"What happened to him?" I asked.

"One day he took off and never came back. Before he vanished, he wrote this book and others, too. So his words and ideas live on."

As we were about to leave, Grandfather leaned in at the window and whispered to me, "That was Hugh's favorite book."

Mom and I finished *The Little Prince* that week. All the while she read to me, I thought about what Grandfather had said. After we read the last page, I asked, "What was Uncle Hugh like? Grandfather said this was his favorite book."

"I really can't tell you very much," she said. "Remember, he died before I was born. I think it was some kind of accident, but your grandfather and grandmother never talked about it. I think it hurt them too much to remember."

"Then why did he tell me this was Uncle Hugh's favorite book?"

"Maybe he's finally coming to terms with it now," Mom said. She took me by the shoulders, the way she did when she was explaining something really important. "It may be hard for you to understand, but you mustn't push him about Uncle Hugh. Give him time. I think he will tell you when he's ready."

"Sort of like how I could use Hugh's room when I had proved myself?" I asked. "How do I do that?"

"You will know when the time comes," Mom said. Then she changed the subject and wouldn't talk about it anymore.

I saw Grandfather Kneale two more times that year. He came to our place for Thanksgiving, and we went over to his house on Christmas morning. Mrs. Phelps and Jason were there also. There were full Christmas stockings for Jason and me hanging from the mantle of the big fireplace in the front room.

"Right where I used to find mine on Christmas morning!" Mom said as I made a grab for it. "How did Santa know?"

I was getting old enough to have doubts about Santa's identity, but I knew enough to keep my mouth shut. Mom and Dad enjoyed it, and I liked the presents. Grandfather was smiling. His smiles were special because he didn't smile often.

Then Mom said something that gave me another clue about Grandfather's past. "How's the book coming, Dad?" she asked as I finished digging the goodies out of the stocking.

"Slowly," Grandfather admitted. "If I'd realized how big a job it was going to be, I probably would never have started it. But now that I'm in, I'll see it through to the end."

"Honestly, Dad!" Mom scolded. "You have to get yourself a computer. Using that old typewriter for such a huge manuscript. . . and it's not even electric! You are absolutely pre-tech!"

"That old typewriter has turned out many a manuscript before this one," Grandfather replied. "Just remember, I was a professor long before I became a priest."

"But where do you find the time?"

Grandfather smiled again. "That's one thing I don't have to worry about," he said. "I'm pretty much retired now. I only teach one class at the seminary and fill in as a supply priest every now and then. If I live long enough, I'll find the time."

On the way back home I asked Mom what a supply priest was.

"It's someone who fills in when the regular priest is sick or on vacation," she explained. "Sort of like a substitute teacher."

That reminded me of something else he had said. "Did Grandfather say he taught at a cemetery?" I asked. Dad laughed so hard he nearly ran the car off the road.

"You're pretty close to being right," he finally said. Mom glared at him.

"No, Jack," she said. "A seminary is where people study to become priests or ministers. A cemetery is where dead people are buried."

"As I said, not much difference," Dad commented.

"Your father is having one of his moods where he thinks he's funny," Mom informed me. "Your grandfather was a professor at a regular college before he became a priest. His subject was ancient history, and he was very good at it. Now he teaches the same course at the seminary." She looked at Dad as if daring him to make another comment. Dad said nothing.

I remembered what Jason had said last summer in the backyard. It was like Grandfather Kneale came from another time, like he really had lived a hundred or even a thousand years ago.

The rest of my first grade year went by. I could read a year or so above grade level by June, but my printing was sloppy and I had a hard time staying inside the lines when I colored. I decided staying inside the lines was boring anyway.

Something important happened that spring. It was right near the end of the school year, May 17, 1987. The *U.S.S. Stark*, a guided missile frigate, was hit by two missiles from an Iraqi aircraft. One exploded and killed 37 American sailors.

Most Americans forgot about it after a day or two, but I remember because Grandfather called us that night right after the news. He talked with Mom first, and I heard her say, "Oh, Dad! It was just a tragic mistake. They didn't mean to do us any harm."

I couldn't hear Grandfather's voice, but I guess he didn't think so. Then he asked to speak to me.

"Did you hear about the attack on the *Stark*?" he asked.

"Yes," I said. "Mom says it was an accident."

"I think it was more like a test," Grandfather said. "I spent five years living and working in Iraq. The people are mostly good, but their leader is a very wicked man. He started a war with Iran that has cost thousands of lives on both sides."

I wondered why Grandfather was telling me this. I was just a kid who didn't know anything about the people of Iraq or who their leader was. Grandfather must have sensed what I was thinking.

"You're old enough to be influenced by what people say," he said. "I'm afraid you're going to hear a lot of bad things about Iraq. Don't believe everything you hear."

I was still confused. "What did you mean by a test?" I asked.

"Is there a bully at your school?" he asked.

"There's one. I hate him."

"Imagine the bully running the school and doing anything he wants. Saddam Hussein, that's the bully, runs Iraq. He has all the power. So what does he want? More power. How does he get it? By gobbling up the little countries around him. How does he do that? By testing them first to see if they'll fight back."

"But why would he pick a fight with us? We're supposed to be the strongest country on earth."

"Like any bully, he's afraid of a real fight. He wants to see if we'll let him get away with what he did. He'll apologize, and probably have the pilot shot. But I'll bet he ordered the attack."

I still couldn't follow what was happening. This was the first time an adult had talked to me about something really serious and treated me like I could understand it. That was when I decided that I really loved my grandfather.

On the last day of school I asked when I could go to Grandfather Kneale's house again. "What?" Mom asked teasingly. "You don't want to go see Grandma and Grandpa Brooks?"

"I can see them anytime," I said. "Besides, I have to share them with my cousins. There aren't any cousins on the Kneale side. At least, not any first cousins!" I was very proud that I now knew what cousins were and what made first cousins different from second cousins.

"You're right," Mom answered. "But his class won't end for another two weeks. Right now he's probably busy grading papers. Let's wait until he's done. And then we'll set a time."

We did and I got to go around the end of June. The old house looked the same, but Grandfather seemed thinner and Mrs. Phelps fatter. Jason was there, too, and stayed for dinner. Mrs. Phelps asked me about school and stuff, but you can tell when grownups are talking to you just to be polite and don't really care what you answer. Grandfather never spoke unless he had something to say. "Have you done any more work on Spud's adventures?" I asked him. Of course, Jason wanted to know who Spud was, so I had to explain. After I finished telling him everything I remembered, he just shrugged and went back to his meatloaf and beans.

"Oh, he's just a story then," he said.

"He's not just a story!" I replied hotly. "He's my story! I even helped think him up, didn't I?" I turned to Grandfather for support. He put down his fork and stroked his chin thoughtfully. "Yes, you did," he admitted. "But, Jack, you can't own a story the way you own a dog or a baseball. It belongs to anyone who can remember and retell it."

I didn't much like that idea. So I decided from then on I would keep Spud's adventures a secret between Grandfather and myself. If Jason asked about them again, I'd just say I forgot. But I wouldn't forget them. Not really. Not ever.

Grandfather must have guessed my feelings, because he said nothing more until Jason and his grandmother had left and I was ready for bed.

"I'm surprised you remembered so much," he told me then. "I think you know the story better than I do. Maybe you should be telling it to me."

"No way!" I said. "You do the telling, and I'll do the remembering." An awful thought struck me. "You did work on them, didn't you?" I asked hopefully.

He gave me another rare smile and said, "Yes. I did."

"Good! Tell me!"

Grandfather stroked his chin again. "Let's see," he muttered. "Where did we leave off?"

"Spud's island was just about to bump into something. Something big like a country or a. . . a. . ."

"Continent, perhaps?" Grandfather suggested.

"Yeah! Like Asia or Africa or America!"

"Which one would you like it to be?"

"Doesn't matter to me. You're telling the story."

"Then I won't say which one it was. Maybe it doesn't exist anymore. Maybe it never existed at all."

"How can that be?" I asked.

"Spud's island could travel through time as well as space, so it can do anything we want it to."

"Then tell me what it did," I said, and Grandfather went on with the story.

Chapter Six

*In which Spud rescues the world's smallest
giant and finds a strange new use for a sheepskin*
. . . .

The ground trembled as another earthquake rocked the kingdom. This time Spud was careful to stand clear of the stump. The tremor shook him off his feet, but he stayed conscious. With one last mighty thump, the earthquake stopped and the fog at the edge of the land cleared away.

"Where are we?" Spud asked as he got to his feet.

"A grim and unfortunate place," Brokenwing said. "I don't much like the look of it."

Spud agreed. The land they were now part of was bleak and barren. Snow-covered hills stretched away toward jagged, icy peaks. Spud could see no trees, no plants, nothing that seemed to be living. The air was quickly growing colder. He shivered.

"I don't like this!" he said. "Let's get the plow and cut our way free."

"Wait, Your Spudship," Brokenwing urged. "All things have a purpose. There must be a reason why we came here. Let's find out what it is."

"You mean you want us to explore this place?"

"Someone or something is out there," Brokenwing reasoned. "Let's explore before we are explored. If we invade before we're invaded, we'll have more choices when we find whatever we're meant to find. Do you have any winter clothing? It's going to be cold."

"Will had an old cloak and hood that was cut down to fit Tom," Spud answered. "Reckon it would just about fit me now."

"I suggest you get it and arm yourself. It might also be a good idea to take water and some mud from the springs. Your mother kept some jars and flasks in her kitchen. They should do."

Spud quickly found the cloak, filled a flask with water and a small jar with mud, took up his shield and nobbeltynook, set Brokenwing on his shoulder and marched toward the border of his kingdom. The fog had vanished, and he could see the sea on three sides of his realm.

The stream now ran from this strange new land to the ocean. Spud stopped to taste the water and found it fresh and very cold. He pulled the cloak tighter about him and marched on. At the border he saw the furrow mark and stepped over it into the unknown land. The invading army of Messy Potatoes, a boy and a talking bird, tramped toward the snow-topped hills.

Spud searched the land for signs of life, but he saw nothing but some moss growing on a few rocks. There were no footprints, no droppings, nothing to indicate that humans or animals had passed that way. The sky overhead was empty of birds.

"Has anything ever lived here?" he wondered. "I don't even see bugs. Why have we come?"

"Something is here for us to find. Keep alert! Whatever is going to happen will happen very soon! I can feel it!"

It can't happen too soon for me, Spud thought as he scrambled up a slope in knee-deep snow. The cloak kept his upper body warm, but his feet felt like he had two pieces of frozen meat in his boots. "Nothing to see but snow and rocks and nothing to hear but wind," he grumbled as they reached the top. Brokenwing, enjoying a free ride, clacked his beak in sympathy.

"What do you expect us to find?" Spud demanded.

"I don't. . . Hark! Listen! That could be it! Do you hear it?"

Spud stopped and rubbed his ears gently. They were so cold he was afraid a brisk rubbing would snap them off his head. Then he listened as hard as he could, but there was nothing but the wind and. . . and something else! Something almost inaudible.

"What's that?" he asked. "I can't quite make it out. Where's it coming from?"

"Over there, I think." Brokenwing pointed left with his beak. "I can't tell what it is, but it sounds like it's in trouble."

"Then let's find out!" Spud said as he started down the slope. Going down wasn't much easier than climbing up. The loose rocks under the snow gave way beneath his weight. Twice he lost his balance and nearly fell on his face.

They were heading in the right direction. The sound was louder now, and it seemed almost human. Something or some-one was in pain and moaning for help.

"Just over that ridge, I believe," said Brokenwing.

Spud climbed cautiously to the ridgetop, dropped to his knees in the snow and peered over the edge. Directly below him lay the biggest man he had ever seen!

"It's a giant!" he whispered in awe.

"Not quite, but almost," Brokenwing replied. "The poor fellow is more than half-dead. Do we help him?"

Spud had heard stories about giants when he was little. In the tales Ma told they were always mean and cruel and fond of eating boys and girls for breakfast. But Spud had a kind heart, and the sight of any creature in pain was enough to make him forget his fear and act. He scrambled down the ridge, with the raven digging in talons to keep its perch.

When Spud reached the bottom, he saw that Brokenwing was right. This critter was a bit too small to be a true giant, but he was far larger than any man Spud had ever met. This particular half-giant would stand just over nine feet tall.

He wasn't exactly standing, though; he couldn't. He was half-sitting, half-lying against a shelf of frozen rock at the foot of the ridge. His hands and feet were bound with thick rope, and his clothes lay in a heap beside him. Close by lay a huge sheep. The sheep was obviously dead, and the half-giant nearly so.

"What is all this?" Spud asked, but the half-giant rolled his eyes, cringed as if in fright and made several low, moaning sounds.

"Look, I want to help!" Spud continued. "Who put you here?"

The half-giant mumbled a few words in a language Spud could not understand and looked more frightened.

"Is he afraid of me?" Spud asked.

"I believe he is," Brokenwing said. "You must look as strange to him as he does to you."

The half-giant cringed and tried to pull away as Spud drew closer, but his back seemed frozen to the rock. When Spud got within a few feet, he noticed the poor critter's back *was* frozen to the rock, and he was too weak to pull himself free.

"I wish I could understand him," Spud said as the half-giant moaned again and tried to speak. The language reminded Spud of someone trying to clear his throat. "How can I help when I don't know why he's here or who did this to him?"

At the back of Spud's mind lurked the thought that perhaps this was an evil monster being justly punished for some terrible deed. But he doubted it. The poor critter looked frightened, confused and a little stupid, though there was no hate in his eyes and no wickedness in his features.

"If I give him a nip, Your Spudship, I could understand and translate for you," said Brokenwing. "I'll do it if you will first whack him lightly with the nobbeltynook. It will help calm him down and ease his pain."

"Right!" said Spud. "One little love tap, just for luck!"

He approached carefully from behind, darted in and rapped the half-giant on the back of his head. The moaning stopped and the head dropped forward. For an instant Spud feared he had struck too hard and killed him. He had never used the weapon before and had no idea of its power. Then Brokenwing jabbed the huge arm and drew blood, and the half-giant head jerked up and the voice mumbled again.

"What's he saying?" Spud asked.

"He wants to know who we are and what we plan to do with him," Brokenwing reported.

"Tell him we ain't gonna hurt him. We want to help, but we need to know who he is and why he's all tied up out here."

Brokenwing began to speak in the same rumbling, throat-clearing language the half-giant used. They spoke back and forth for quite a while before the raven translated.

"He says that he has no name. The other giants never gave him one because he was so small and puny. Apparently, a giant has to earn his name. He was never given a chance because of his size. In fact, he is considered a midget among giants."

"Biggest dang midget I ever saw!" Spud said as he surveyed the half-giant's nine-foot-plus frame. "Does he mean that his fellow giants would leave him out here to die just because he was smaller than they were? That's just plain low-down dirty!"

Brokenwing spoke, listened and translated. "He says that's part of it. The rest is that he didn't like being cruel and refused to tear folks apart and wouldn't eat girls or boys for breakfast or lunch. . . not even for dinner."

Well, that's encouraging, Spud decided. This must be the reason we came to this awful place. Maybe we can free him and take him with us. A nice, gentle half-giant might come in right handy.

"Tell him we'll help," Spud said.

Again Brokenwing spoke, listened and translated. "He says it's no use. He's stuck to the rock and too weak to free himself, and he's sure that we aren't strong enough either."

"How did he freeze to a rock in the first place?" Spud wondered. "Have you ever heard of people trying to lick iron in freezing weather?" Brokenwing asked. "Their tongues can stick right to it. Well, this rock contains iron ore. They poured water over it and down his back and then held him against it until he stuck fast. We can't pull him loose."

"Maybe if we went back and got Blossom. . ."

"Not enough time," Brokenwing said. "The cold would kill him before we got back. Whatever we do, we must do it now."

Desperately, Spud looked about for something to work with, for an idea, for anything that might help. Again he noticed the sheep. He paid no attention to it before, since it was obviously dead and beyond help. Now he noticed a bundle of wood piled beside it.

"Ask him what the sheep and the wood are for," he said.

"They were put there to make him suffer," the raven translated after listening to the half-giant. "The sheep was his pet, but giants aren't supposed to have pets. So they killed it and put it out here along with the wood and his clothes. The wood could be used for a fire, and the clothes or the hide could keep him warm, but he can't get to them. The idea was for him to freeze slowly while looking at them."

"That's the meanest bit of low-down skunkery I ever heard of!" Spud exclaimed. "But it's not gonna happen! I'm gonna set him free, Brokenwing! You tell him that!"

The raven translated, listened and reported. "He asks how. He's stuck fast."

"I'll make a fire and we'll melt the ice," Spud answered.

"It will also burn all the skin off his back. He would die without any hide, and it would be a slow and painful death."

"Then we'll give him a new hide!" Spud replied as he drew out his knife and tinderbox. "He can be half-man and half-giant and half-sheep!"

"He can't be three halves," Brokenwing said. "You should say a third, a third, and a third. We must work on your arithmetic, Your Spudship. But it is a wonderful idea."

Spud smeared the knife with mud from the three magic springs and was soon busily skinning the sheep. The hide came off quickly and cleanly. Then he kindled a fire and picked up the nobbeltynook.

"I'm going to give him another rap and put him out," he warned. "Tell him when he wakes, he'll be free and have a warm new hide, as well."

As soon as Brokenwing translated, Spud smacked the half-giant hard enough to knock him out, but not (he hoped) hard enough to do any real damage. Then he took a burning stick from the fire, forced it between the half-giant's frozen back and the rock and prayed for his plan to work.

It did. Slowly the captive peeled away from the rock. But all his skin, from his shoulders down to and including his bottom, remained behind. The smell was awful.

Spud grabbed the sheepskin, trimmed it, smeared on the mud as a sort of glue and laid it over the burned area. He cut several more strips from the hide and used them to tie the new skin in place until the mud had time to harden.

"It looks kinda weird, but I think it might work," he said.

The half-giant twitched and moaned, opened his eyes, and then realized he was free from the rock. Spud cut the rope binding his feet. He started to cut the rope binding the arms, then hesitated. A half-giant was half a giant, after all, and giants had very bad reputations. This half-giant said he was not like the others, but how far could his word be trusted?

"What do you think?" he asked Brokenwing.

"I suggest we trust his word," said the raven. "He must be the reason why we came. But make haste! The others may come back, and we don't want to be around when they do!"

Spud cut the remaining ropes and helped the half-giant to his feet. "Ask him if he's strong enough to walk," he said.

"He says he is," Brokenwing reported. "He will go anywhere you ask and serve you for all his days. He asks only that you give him a name."

"Oh, all right," said Spud. He thought a moment and said, "I name you Malcolm." He wasn't sure why he picked that name, but it seemed to fit. Then he had another idea.

"One name ain't enough for someone your size," he told the half-giant. "You oughta have a second one that kinda describes you. He looked over the strange creature with his new sheep hide and said, "Malcolm Woolybottom! That's gonna be your name!"

"Mall-coome Wool-ee-bot-tom!" rumbled the half-giant.

"Get your duds on, Malcolm," said Spud, pointing to the half-giant's clothes. "I think we need to be leaving these parts!"

Malcolm nodded his understanding and scrambled into his clothes. Spud led the way, backtracking his trail through the snow with Brokenwing on his shoulder. Malcolm followed a few steps behind, even though one of his strides equaled more than two of Spud's. But soon he began to grow nervous.

"He senses something," Brokenwing said. "I fear one of the true giants may have come back to see if he is dead yet. We had better pick up the pace!"

"I can't go any faster! The snow is too deep!"

"Then let him carry us," the raven suggested.

Spud nodded and Brokenwing spoke the command. The half-giant set Spud on one huge shoulder as easily as Spud carried Brokenwing. Spud pointed to the trail and said, "Tell him to follow that, and we'll be back in my land in no time."

"I fear we will need to be, Your Spudship. I can hear noises back there!"

They left the snow just before the border and quickly crossed into the Kingdom of Messy Potatoes. But that was not enough. Giants could cross borders too, and Spud could now hear them coming. Would he have time to cut them free?

"Have Malcolm put us down and hide behind something," Spud ordered. "He'd scare half the life outa Blossom, and we need her to draw the plow!"

Blossom was already waiting by the harness and did not seem a bit disturbed at the sight of a woolly half-giant. Spud had her hitched up and at the border in record time, but the sounds were getting louder and closer. They were very angry sounds, too.

Spud jammed the plowshare into the furrow and urged Blossom forward. "I'm not gonna take one foot of this blasted land!" he vowed. Not an inch! Not a pebble! Not even a grain of sand! Just let us get away, Lord! That's all I ask!"

Spud didn't know much about praying, but Ma said it sometimes worked. And this time it did.

Spud felt the earth begin to shake as he cut the last few rods. As he pulled the plowshare free, the tremor increased and he dropped to his knees. So did Blossom. The earth began to split along the furrow. The split grew wider, and water rushed in to fill it. They were free and drifting!

Just before the fog blotted out the horizon, Spud caught a glimpse of several giants standing on the far shore, waving their fists and bellowing curses (or at least that's what he thought they were).

Then the fog settled around the island like a curtain, and they were floating on the sea once more.

Chapter Seven

In which Spud survives an encounter with
Little Red Riding Hood and decides to rescue the wolf
instead
• • • • • • • • • • • • • • • •

"Quark!" called the raven two mornings later as he hopped onto Spud's bed in the Royal Cottage of Messy Potatoes.

"Mmmph!" mumbled a sleepy King Spud as he slowly opened one eye. "Good morning, Brokenwing. I see the sun is up. Have you got any news?"

"Quark!"

Spud's arm appeared from beneath the quilt. "This had better be important," he warned. "I don't much like being stabbed just to have someone to chat with."

"Quark!" the raven repeated and then jabbed.

"Ouch! All right, what news, you bloodthirsty bird? This is our third day adrift. Are we going to strike land soon?"

"The fog shows signs of thinning, Your Spudship," Brokenwing reported. We should strike another land mass sometime today."

"Then I suppose I'd better get up and see about break-fast," Spud said as he rubbed his eyes and crawled out of bed. "You got any idea where this wine dark sea of yours is taking us this time?"

"None whatever," said the raven as Spud pulled on his tunic and britches, grabbed the shield and nobbeltynook and set out, with Brokenwing on his shoulder, to survey his king-dom. The raven was right. The fog was thinning just a bit.

Beyond the field of messy potatoes and the old stump with the magic springs, in a direction that once had been west, Malcolm Woolybottom and Blossom were plowing a field. Spud was never sure what season they might sail into, but he wanted to keep the half-giant as busy as he could while letting the others get used to him. Blossom had taken to Malcolm immediately. Maybe the sheepskin smell had helped. But Old Tom had run off to the woods and hadn't been seen for three days.

The new hide was working well. Malcolm's fleece was thick and even showed signs of growing. Spud had cut out the back of his shirt and britches, since they hardly seemed necessary, and Malcolm would have to be shorn two or three times a year. The half-giant was a good worker and trying hard to learn Spud's language.

Spud smeared some mud on the wound that Brokenwing had given him. The mixture healed it in a few hours. The raven's daily advice and conversation came at a price.

"Sure wish I knew where and when we was going," Spud said as he scanned the fog along the horizon. Overhead the sun was bright, but traveling in a direction that had been south to north. He could feel the gentle motion of the land as it bobbed up and down on the sea, which, when it could be seen, wasn't wine dark at all.

"That's the wonder of it," said the raven. "But if you know who you are, *how* you are and *why* you are, then the where and the when don't matter so much."

"New law for this land: no philosophy before breakfast," Spud said. "Go help Malcolm with his language lessons while I try to find us some fish."

Spud followed the fog along the shoreline. The curtain was only a few feet thick, and flying fish often landed beyond it and lay in the open waiting to be picked up. One or two were enough for Spud, but Malcolm could easily put down a dozen at one sitting and be hungry again by midday.

Spud had gathered a few fish when he saw a familiar form crouching at the edge of the fog. Old Tom was out hunting for breakfast, too.

"Hey, Tom, are you a fisherman now?" Spud asked as he stroked the cat's fur. Old Tom looked up from his half-eaten fish and meowed. He was not happy with the way things were, but he allowed Spud to pet him while he ate.

"You don't like the new folks, eh? I'll bet you miss Ma, too. So do I, but we're stuck on this island until we get someplace else. You're just gonna have to make the best of it along with the rest of us. Why don't you try making friends with Brokenwing and Malcolm? They're nice folks, once you get to know them."

Old Tom gave Spud a look of disgust that only an offended cat can give and stalked off into the fog, twitching his tail in anger. "Guess he thinks that's a bad idea," Spud decided.

Spud returned to his Royal Cottage with fifteen fish and began fixing breakfast for his subjects. "Bet I'm the only king in history who's also his country's chief cook," he said as he worked in the kitchen. "Be nice to have a real cook take over the job. Maybe the next land we hit will have one we can borrow."

The thought made him run outside and whistle for his subjects. The fog was thinning out, and he didn't like the idea of ramming another continent on an empty stomach. Malcolm Woolybottom, with the raven on his shoulder, came at a run. Spud carried a huge platter of food outside to him, since the half-giant was far too big to fit into the cottage. He flipped half a fish to Brokenwing and then joined his subjects outside. King and servant ate with their fingers and wiped their mouths on their sleeves, which were not very clean to begin with and which grew dirtier and smellier with every meal.

"Fish good!" Malcolm rumbled. "King Spud good cook!"

"He's getting better," Brokenwing said. "For somebody stupid, he's really quite smart. In another month we can start on manners. . .for both of you!" he added as Spud blew his nose on the same sleeve he had used for wiping his mouth.

Before Spud could reply, the ground shook and the fog disappeared completely. The Kingdom of Messy Potatoes swiveled a bit and then thumped into a larger land mass. Spud picked up his shield and the nobbeltynook.

"Stay here and guard the cottage," he told Malcolm. "Have Blossom harnessed and ready to plow in case we need to get out in a hurry. Come on, Brokenwing! Let's see what kind of land we've bumped into this time!"

King Spud and his feathered advisor stepped across the furrow and into an unknown land. "This sure beats the last place!" Spud said as they paused to look around. "Leastwise, it ain't freezing this time."

The land was nearly flat, with just a few low hills, and heavily forested. Spud saw several paths leading into the woods in different directions. "Which one should we take?" he asked.

Brokenwing ruffled his feathers uneasily. He did not seem happy with the land. "You are the king. You make the choice," he said.

"I choose this one," Spud said. "It's the nearest and the widest, so I figure it's the one we're meant to take."

"Maybe and maybe not," said the raven. "I sense an enemy."

The sun had the warmth of late spring. The trees wore fresh new leaves. Spud could hear the songs of birds and the scurrying of small animals in the undergrowth. There was life all around him and adventure up ahead. He felt completely happy, so why was Brokenwing feeling so uneasy?

They had walked about a mile when Spud heard something heavy crashing through the underbrush. He tightened his grip on the nobbeltynook. Was it a bear?

It wasn't. To his amazement, Spud saw an old woman break through the undergrowth and run down the path toward them. "Help! Oh help, kind Sir!" she cried.

"What's wrong?" Spud asked as she stood panting before him.

"It. . . it's my granddaughter!" the old woman gasped. "She's in great danger! I must find help quickly! Are you a woodsman?"

"Well, I'm in the woods right now, so I guess you could say so. What's the danger?"

"It's a wolf!" the old woman cried.

"Did it carry her off? When? Which way did they go?"

"It hasn't got her yet, but it plans to! Come quickly!"

The old woman darted back into the underbrush. Spud followed as fast as he could, but this old granny could run pretty well for someone her age. He had a hard time keeping up. At last she stopped and pointed ahead to a clearing.

"There. . . in my little house!" she gasped.

"Your granddaughter's in there?" Spud asked.

"No, you ninny!" the old woman snapped. "The wolf's in there waiting in ambush! We've got to warn her!"

"Why do you need me for that? I'm a stranger in these parts. I don't know who your granddaughter is!"

"There are two paths from her mother's house to mine, and I don't know which one she took," the old woman said. "If I choose the wrong one, she'll walk straight into the wolf's mouth! You cover one and I'll take the other. We've got to warn her!"

For some reason the old woman's story sounded familiar to Spud. "How will I know her? What does she look like?" he asked.

"How many little girls do you expect to find on a path in the middle of a forest?" the old woman replied. "She's very pretty, a bit smaller than you, and probably carrying a basket of goodies for me. And she usually wears a bright red hood. It goes well with her complexion."

"All right. I'll cover this path. You take the other one. If I see her, what. . ."

But the old woman had already ducked back into the undergrowth. Brokenwing nervously clacked his beak.

"I was afraid something like this might happen," he commented. "Beware, Your Spudship! These currents run deep."

"What currents? We're on dry land in the middle of a forest."

"Does all this remind you of a tale you've heard before?"

"Yeah. It's an old story Ma told me when I was little. I never could figure how a wolf could talk or how a girl could mistake a wolf in a nightgown for her own grandmother. Sometimes I thought she was blind, and sometimes I thought she was just awfully stupid. What do you think it was?"

"I think you will soon find out for yourself," Brokenwing said. "Here she comes now!"

The girl skipping down the path looked just like the Little Red Riding Hood Spud had imagined when he closed his eyes while Ma was telling her story. Her hood was really a cape and bonnet. Under it she wore a white dress that came to her ankles. Her hair and eyes were dark. She eyed Spud with a bored, vacant smile.

"Oh, hello," she said in a high, toneless voice.

"'Lo yourself," said Spud. "Are you Little Red Riding Hood?"

"People sometimes call me that," the girl replied. "That's because it's so bright and pretty, just like I am."

"Are you on your way to your grandmother's house?"

"Yes. Poor Granny has been so sick lately. Mama sent me with this basket of goodies to cheer her up. But I don't think she needs it. Just the sight of me would cheer anyone up, right?"

"Listen," said Spud. "Did you just meet anyone?"

"Yes I did!" the girl replied. "He asked me where I was going with the basket and was so *awfully* concerned that I was traveling alone. He was *such* a polite gentleman too, with big dark eyes and curious ears and. . ."

"That was no gentleman!" Spud interrupted. "That was a wolf! He's waiting for you at your grandma's house right now, and he plans to eat you for dinner!"

"Oh!" said the girl in the same high, toneless voice. "Whatever shall I do?"

"Let me take care of it," Spud urged. "Change clothes with me, give me your basket, and wait here with this raven. I'll deal with the wolf."

The girl looked at Spud's dirty, wrinkled tunic and worn, stained britches and shuddered. "You want me to put *those* on?" she said, wrinkling her nose. "They're a boy's clothes! They're years out of style, and they haven't been washed for weeks!"

"How do you think I'm gonna feel in a dress?" Spud responded. "But if you'd rather walk around without anything, that's your choice. You go behind that tree. I'll go behind this one, and we'll toss the stuff to each other."

"Oh, very well," the girl replied. She disappeared behind a large oak. Presently the dress and hood sailed out from behind the tree and landed at Spud's feet. He gathered them up, ducked behind another tree and lobbed the tunic and britches over to her. The dress was a tight fit, but he finally got it on.

A hoodless Red Riding Hood stumbled out from behind the oak with her hands under the tunic to hold the britches up. "These things are *disgusting*!" she cried.

Spud was in a hurry. "Now, help me tie this hood on, and I'll go take care of the wolf."

"Don't you *dare* get any blood on my good dress when you kill it!" the girl warned. "It never washes out!"

"I'll try to be careful," Spud promised as he picked up the basket and nobbeltynook. He was puzzled. Girls were supposed to be grateful when you saved them. Would the girl he had glimpsed at Count Rolph's behave this way too? Something was wrong. . .

Grandma's house also looked just as it had in his mind, right down to the bed in one corner. The creature in the bed was definitely a wolf, and yet somehow it did look just a bit like an old lady. Spud recalled the storyteller who was not a real storyteller, and how Brokenwing was not a real raven. Was this more of the tempter's magic? Was it another test?

"Look, Grandma!" he called in a voice pitched as high as he could. "I brought some goodies to help you feel better."

"How sweet of you, my child!" The words seemed to come from the wolf's mouth, yet Spud sensed it wasn't the wolf who was speaking. "Come closer so I can see you."

I've heard that voice before, Spud thought as he approached and said, "Why Grandma, what big eyes you have!"

"All the better to see you with!" the voice replied.

"And Grandma! What big ears you have!" Spud continued as he thought, not a wolf, not a grandma, so what is it?

"All the better to hear you with, my dear!"

"And Grandma! What a long nose you have!"

"Why, all the better to smell you with, my dear!"

The storyteller's voice! The tempter had used him and now was using the wolf! No wonder Brokenwing sensed trouble! Spud tightened his grip on the nobbeltynook he held behind his back and said, "And Grandma! What big, sharp teeth you have!"

"All the better to eat you with, my dear!" snarled the wolf as it leaped from the bed. Spud brought the nobbeltynook around in a swing that caught the wolf on the side of its head and dropped it in mid-spring like an empty sack. As it fell, Spud heard a rushing sound. Something invisible sped past him and out the door. Then everything was quiet.

So much for the tempter, he thought. Now for the wolf!

A quick search of Grandma's cupboards turned up a length of stout rope. Spud used the knife he had slipped into the basket to cut pieces to bind the wolf's legs and tie its muzzle shut. Then he grabbed the scruff of its neck and dragged it up the path to where Red Riding Hood waited.

"What a disgusting creature!" she cried. "Do you mean it was going to lay its filthy paws on *me*?"

"Paws and claws and jaws, as well," Spud agreed.

"You didn't harm the dress, did you? It took Mama weeks to make it!"

"Just a little sweat and maybe a spot or two of dirt."

"Then pul-*eeze* give it back! You're a wonderful woodsman, but your clothes are disgusting!"

"Actually, I'm not a woodsman," Spud confessed. "I'm. . . well. . . more like a king."

"Really?" the girl said from behind the oak as she threw Spud's dirty tunic and britches back to him. "With castles and servants and royal coaches?" Her voice took on a new and very different tone. "I understand! You're disguised as a woodsman to prove yourself. How noble of you!"

"Not quite," Spud admitted. "See, I'm just a starting-out king, so my kingdom's not big enough for castles and coaches yet. But it's gonna grow! It's really gonna be something someday!"

"Hmmm," said Red Riding Hood as she reappeared in her dress and hood. She looked Spud over carefully. "You don't seem to be rich or well-born, and you certainly do need a bath. But you did save my life, and you are rather cute in an odd sort of way. So perhaps I just might be persuaded."

"Persuaded to do what?" asked a puzzled Spud.

"Why, marry you, of course! Haven't you read any of the stories? The beautiful girl. . .that's me. . .*always* marries the handsome prince. . . I guess that's you. . .after he rescues her, and they live happily ever after!"

This was news to Spud, who had never even had a chance to flirt with Count Rolph's servant girls. "I. . .I think I'm a little too young to get married," he stammered.

"Age has nothing to do with it," said Red Riding Hood. "I'm probably younger than you are anyway."

"But. . ."

Red Riding Hood scowled. She was not used to people with other ideas. "If you saved my life and if you are a king, as you claim, then you *have* to marry me and we *have* to live happily ever after! It's the law in this land!"

"Not where I come from!" argued Spud.

"But that's not where you are now! You obey the laws of the land you're in, and the laws of this land say that the handsome prince must marry the beautiful maiden after he rescues her. Do you know how many times I've hiked through these woods waiting for this to happen? Poor Grandma doesn't even *like* the stuff in this basket! Now give me a kiss and we'll start planning the wedding."

"Uh, what about the wolf?" Spud asked.

"He can be part of the ceremony," Red Riding Hood decided. "We shall have him roasted alive on our wedding day as a warning to other wolves that beautiful maidens in this land are not to be eaten, torn asunder, or molested in any other way. Let's go. Mama will want to meet you."

"Wait!" Spud cried. "I'm all sweaty, I need a bath and you know what my clothes are like. Let me run back to my kingdom and clean up. I'll meet you back here in an hour."

Red Riding Hood was a little suspicious. "You're going to leave me alone with this wolf?"

"I'll take him with me," Spud offered. "We can't just leave him here. There's sure to be a law against leaving wolves tied up along public pathways. We'll keep him secure and helpless in my kingdom until the day of the big wedding and wolf roast."

Red Riding Hood still looked suspicious, so Spud seized the wolf by the neck and pointed to its tail. "Could you grab the other end so we can carry him between us?"

"Ugh!" she exclaimed. "You want me to *touch* that creature? To get wolf hairs and wolf sweat all over my beautiful clothes? Get him out of here! I'll wait for you at Granny's." She forced a smile and added, "My dear."

Spud picked up Brokenwing and headed for the border. "I hope Blossom is ready to plow," he muttered. "The sooner we're outa here the better!"

"What about the wolf?" Brokenwing asked.

"What about him? You don't expect me to free him, do you?"

"No. Once the tempter has been in him, he's worthless as a wolf. He knows too much about mankind now. Still, to be roasted alive just because the tempter used him. . ."

"All right," Spud said. "We'll take him with us just for a while. Malcolm can carry him back and keep him secure until we reach a new land. Then we'll turn him loose."

"You may not want to. Dogs, even wolves, have a way of attaching themselves to people."

"Not to me!" Spud insisted. "I don't want a wolf for a pet any more than I want to get married! Not now and not ever!" Then he thought of the girl he had glimpsed at Count Rolph's castle and added, "Well, *probably* not ever!"

Chapter Eight

*In which Spud gains land, loses land,
and deals with visitors who come by night*
· · · · · · · · · · · · · · · ·

"Puppy!" Malcolm rumbled when he saw the bound-up
wolf lying on the path. "King Soud get puppy for Malcolm!"
He picked up the wolf with one hand and draped it around his
neck. The wolf squirmed and snarled but could no nothing
else.

"Malcolm," Spud said. "That's not a puppy. That's a
wolf!"

"Wolf," Malcolm repeated. "Good name for puppy!" He
set off down the trail for Spud's land, happy as a child with a
new pet.

"What do we do now?" Spud asked Brokenwing.

"I suggest we leave as quickly as possible," said the raven.
"Any land that roasts wolves alive for wedding celebrations
will have very nasty ways of dealing with unwilling bride-
grooms."

As they stepped across the furrow, Spud wondered, "What
would have happened if I'd taken one of the other paths?"

"On one you would have found a house owned by three
bears and a breaking and entering girl you would have felt
compelled to rescue. Another would lead to a house where a
girl sits among cinders and dreams about going to a dance."

"I know those stories, but I don't want to live them. Let's
cut our way out of here."

The wolf terrified Blossom. She rolled her eyes in fear
and refused to approach until Malcolm carried it out of sight.

Only then would she allow herself to be led to the furrow.

"Do you want to take a piece of this land with you?" Brokenwing asked. "It is enchanted, after all."

"Maybe just a bit. It would be nice to have a forest."

"Remember, whatever it contains is yours, for good or for ill."

Spud smeared mud on the plowshare, set the plow in the furrow and Blossom began to cut his kingdom free from the strange land. Halfway across the cut, he swung Blossom to the left and cut a new furrow through the woods. The plowshare turned the soft earth quickly. Spud tried to keep his own land in sight, but soon lost track of it. Each tree, each shrub pulled him farther and farther to the left.

"Take care, Your Spudship! I hear voices!"

Spud turned the plow sharply right and flicked the reins for more speed. Blossom picked up her pace and Spud, too, heard voices, angry, threatening voices coming his way!

"What do they want?" he asked Brokenwing.

"They want you. This is the land of stories, and you have broken one of their themes. Their themes are their laws, and you are a. . . well. . . a variant. That makes you a criminal in their eyes."

"I'm not a criminal! I just don't want to get married yet!"

The voices grew louder, but the old furrow was in sight. Spud drove Blossom as hard as he could. They cut across the old furrow as the voices behind them swelled to a roar. The land shook, the earth split, and the sea poured in once more.

Spud admired the new addition as the fog closed in around his kingdom. He had gained a little over an acre, stuck onto what had once been the northeast corner. The way the land gently revolved as it bobbed on the sea, it could just as easily be the southwest.

It was good land, whatever its direction. He decided to name it Hood's Woods, in memory of the girl he had saved and nearly had to marry. Now all he needed was a few more subjects. . .

The thought reminded him that he did have one more subject, with four legs, very sharp teeth, and a nasty disposition.

What was he going to do with the wolf? It might be days before they struck another land. He decided to seek Brokenwing's advice.

"You have a problem here," the raven said as he watched Malcolm Woolybottom cradle the beast in his arms and gently stroke its fur. The wolf had stopped struggling, but it glared at the half-giant with a pair of hard, yellow, unfriendly eyes. "He wants to untie it and make it a pet."

"I'll let him free its muzzle," Spud decided. "After it chomps him two or three times, he may change his mind."

For someone with fists the size of melons, Malcolm Woolybottom had very nimble fingers. He soon had Spud's knots untied and the wolf's jaws were free. It immediately snapped at him.

"No, Puppy!" Malcolm said as he gently (for a half-giant) cuffed it on the side of its head. "You no bite Malcolm!" The wolf whined and allowed Malcolm to go on petting it.

"Can he actually tame it?" Spud wondered.

"You whacked it with the nobbeltynook. That drove a lot of the nastiness out of it. Dogs bond quickly with new masters. Maybe a wolf will too. I suggest you let Malcolm try."

"But the tempter has been in it. . ."

"A tempter never cares for anyone or anything. He only uses them while it suits him. When they're of no further use, he leaves for someone or something else. Did you feel anything when you whacked the wolf?"

"Yes," said Spud. "A sound like something rushing past me, but I couldn't see anything."

"You never see the tempter, just the results of what he does. Sometimes you can fix things, and sometimes you can't. Maybe this time we can."

"It's probably hungry. I'll get some more fish. I want him well-fed, Brokenwing. This land is too small for Blossom and a hungry wolf!"

"Already you are making wise decisions," said the raven. "But let Malcolm do it. The wolf must know who its master is."

The half-giant set off on his fishing trip, with the wolf tucked securely under one arm. Meanwhile, Spud turned his attention to what might happen when they struck land again. Most kings knew where they were, who their neighbors were and how friendly or unfriendly they might be. Spud's kingdom could run into anyone, anywhere, any time.

Or anyone could run into him, as he was about to find out.

Late that very night, Spud was awakened in his Royal Cottage by a slight thump. He opened his eyes and listened, but heard and felt nothing. The land gently bobbed on the sea. They must still be adrift, he thought. What had they hit? Or what had hit them?

He heard a ruffling of feathers, and a voice beside him said, "Quark!"

"You felt it too, Brokenwing? What was it?"

"Quark!"

"Oh, all right, you bloodthirsty bird! Jab away! Ouch!"

"My apologies, Your Spudship. I think we've been invaded."

"How? We're drifting. I can feel us bobbing up and down."

"Ships sail the sea and some are careless or foolish enough to sail into fog. Someone has rammed us. I fear they are run hard aground and stuck fast."

"Who could they be?" Spud wondered.

"They could be anyone. We had better find out."

"Can't it wait until morning?" Spud complained.

"They might not wait for morning. We'd better not either."

So Spud roused himself, put on his still-unwashed clothes, placed the raven on his shoulder and set out to see who had hit them. The night was clear, with a full moon and a sky full of stars. Whoever hit them must have seen the fog bank. Why did they sail into it?

"Should I try to wake Malcolm?" Spud asked as they stepped outside. The half-giant was one of the world's soundest sleepers. Nothing short of an earthquake or a whack with the nobbeltynook would rouse him before morning.

"Better not until we know what we're facing. He would want to bring the wolf, and I don't trust it yet."

They followed the furrow down from the stump to the shore and began to circle the island, bearing to the right to avoid going widdershins. They had just crossed the stream, now running salt water again, when they saw a light and heard voices.

"They've built a fire, whoever they are," Spud muttered as they drew near. "I hear them talking, but I can't understand the language. Do you know it, Brokenwing?"

"I'm not sure, but it sounds like Norse or Icelandic," said the raven. "I fear they may be Vikings."

They were Vikings. As they drew closer, Spud saw a ship's prow jutting out of the fog and several men gathered around a fire a short distance from it. They wore horned helmets and were filling flagons from a huge barrel. Brokenwing sniffed once and clacked his beak in disgust.

"Mead!" he said. "No wonder they rammed into us! They're drunk, every one of them, and getting drunker by the moment!"

"They also look like they mean to stay a while," Spud observed as he watched men carrying several other barrels ashore. All the carriers hurried over to the open barrel as soon as they had dropped their cargoes.

"There are far too many for us to fight, even with Malcolm and the wolf on our side. You're the king. What do you want to do?"

"If they won't leave us, then we'll have to leave them," Spud replied. "Keep watch while I go get Blossom and the plow."

"You are gaining in wisdom," the raven said approvingly, but Spud was already gone.

He ran as quickly as he could to the shed where Blossom slept, roused her and slipped on the harness. Blossom did not like night work, but something in Spud's manner made her go along with no complaint. Malcolm Woolybottom, who shared the shed with her, snored peacefully through it all.

The wolf, chained to the far wall, watched with hard, yellow eyes but made no sound.

Spud first tried to hurry Blossom. Then he decided to take his time. The Vikings were going into camp for the night. The more they drank, the less alert they would be. Hopefully, most of them would pass out in a short while.

After crossing the stream, Spud stopped and scanned the darkness for Brokenwing. It's not easy to spot a black bird at night. Spud had no idea where the raven was until something pecked at his ankle. "Ouch! You've already had your blood for the day!"

"Ouch yourself, Your Spudship! You nearly stepped on me."

"Anything happen while I was gone?" Spud asked.

"Three fights, four songs, two speeches, and an incredible volume of very powerful mead drunk down coarse and leathery throats," the raven reported. "In short, an average Viking celebration."

"What are they celebrating?"

"I don't know, and I don't think they do either. But the sooner we are rid of them, the better."

Spud set the plowshare in the furrow. Cutting a new line around the camp and setting them adrift would be easy enough if he kept a safe distance between himself and the camp. But the safer the distance, the more land he would lose. On the other hand, the closer he cut, the more he would keep. The closer he cut, the bigger the risk. . .

He flicked the reins and guided Blossom along the furrow toward the camp. He would shave it as close as he could. If he kept quiet and outside the firelight he could slip past and lose only a few rods of land.

The celebration had died down to rumbles and an occasional belch. Most of the crew were lying flat. A few were sitting. None were standing. Spud eased the plowshare out of the furrow and began to cut a new line very close to camp.

Blossom was frightened. He could tell by the way the reins quivered. Or were those his own hands trembling? Nearer and nearer they came. Spud could now smell the Vikings.

The salt and grime on their clothes and skin made his nose twitch, and he nearly sneezed.

A large Viking rolled over and burped. Blossom froze like a statue. The Viking's head lolled from side to side. Then he sighed and began to snore. Spud flicked the reins as gently as he could, and the line around the camp bent toward the old furrow and the sea once again.

They were going to make it! Just a few yards more. . .

Just then a Viking shout disrupted the night: "Guildeflormandt!"

Spud had no idea what the word was, but he knew what it meant. They had been spotted! Someone was awake and trying to raise an alarm!"

"Pull, Blossom!" Spud cried, but the cow needed no urging. She drove straight for the old furrow, and the two lines joined just as a figure leaped from the prow of the ship and dashed toward them, waving an ax and yelling!

Once again the earth shook and split. The tremor made the Viking hesitate. Then he shouted and charged. The sea poured into the split and forced the two islands farther and farther apart.

If the Viking hadn't hesitated, he might have cleared the gap. He wavered just long enough and it was too far. He yelled, waved his arms, and tried to stop his leap. He splashed into the sea just as the Kingdom of Messy Potatoes pulled away from the ship and the little stretch of beach.

As the fog thickened Spud knew the Vikings couldn't get organized and give chase in time. He pulled the plow from the furrow and patted Blossom on the head.

"Good old cow! I'll take you over any plow horse any day!"

Brokenwing appeared out of the night and pecked at Spud's ankle for attention. "That was cutting it a little too close," he said.

"But we did it. We're safe now," Spud reminded him.

"Not quite. Some danger still remains. You had better arm yourself."

Spud wished Brokenwing would be more specific, but he knew the raven was almost always right. He led Blossom back to the shed and took up his shield and the nobbeltynook. Malcolm Woolybottom still snored peacefully, and the wolf continued to stare with its cold, yellow eyes. No sense hunting in the dark, Spud decided. The danger can wait for morning.

The night sky grew lighter as, one by one, the stars winked away. Then the sun rose over the fog to the southwest. Never knowing from which direction the dawn would come always momentarily disoriented Spud. It was like closing his eyes, spinning four or five times in a circle, then opening them again.

Well, time to go hunting for danger. . .

The danger was not hard to find. As he neared the spot where he had cut the kingdom free from the ship, Spud heard someone moaning and thrashing about in the fog. He had missed one Viking in the dark and left him on the wrong side of the furrow!

Spud's first thought was to return for Malcolm Woolybottom and the wolf. The Viking would be big and probably armed as well. "No," he said. "If I am king, then I must set the example and be responsible for the kingdom's safety. I've tamed a half-giant and subdued a wolf. I should be able to handle one lost Viking."

Spud called out, "Hello there! Are you lost?" He knew he would not be understood, but he wanted the Viking to realize that he was not alone. "Come this way! I'm over here!"

"Feoofnafar!" (That might not have been the actual word the Viking spoke, but it sounded something like that.) The Viking blundered out of the fog and stared wildly. He was a lot smaller than Malcolm Woolybottom, but a lot bigger than Spud. His tunic and britches were filthy, even compared to Spud's, and his hair and beard were caked with dirt, salt brine, and other things. His shield and helmet must have gone with the ship, but he still carried his battle-ax, and he looked like he knew how to use it!

Spud put down the nobbeltynook and held up an empty right hand as a sign of peace, but the Viking wanted none of it. He roared something that sounded like, "Leeearrf!" and charged, waving the ax over his head.

I'm doomed! Spud thought as he grabbed up the nobbeltynook and raised his shield to ward off the blow. This little disk of wood can't possibly stop that ax!

But it did! The huge ax struck the shield with a loud "Thonk!" and glanced away. Spud barely felt the shock of the blow. It was like the Viking had whacked him with a piece of straw.

"Leeearrf!" the Viking cried and struck again, and again the blow bounced away harmlessly. Spud took a quick glance at his shield. It had not even been marked!

The Viking still did not give up easily and gathered himself for a third blow. I can't let this go on, Spud thought. Sooner or later he's going to get lucky and get past my guard. I'm going to have to hit back!

As the third blow struck his shield, Spud swung at the Viking's helmetless head. The nobbeltynook connected with a sharp "Thwack!" and the Viking's knees buckled. He swayed, then all his muscles seemed to relax at once and he fell on his face and lay still.

Spud checked to see if he was still breathing. He was. "Well, it looks like I've just gained another subject," he said to the unconscious Viking.

Chapter Nine

In which I hear an important announcement and
learn more about a mysterious uncle
. . . .

These weren't the only stories Grandfather told me. He knew lots of folk tales and made up other stories, too. I remember a few about the skillywidden, a Scottish giant who was kind of stupid.

There were a couple of Manx folk tales. I wanted Spud to go to the Isle of Man, but Grandfather said the Isle was so small that it couldn't afford to lose any more land.

I remember another character called the Hin. I think he was from India. Grandfather always started his stories with a rhyme that went:

> One Hin does.
> Two Hindu.
> You be one.
> You do too.

When I recited it for Mom, she smiled and said, "He made that up for me when I was your age! I'd forgotten all about it."

I think that's why I liked Spud's stories best of all. I knew those were mine and nobody else's. I was really getting interested in them when my time ran out for the summer. Grandfather had to fly back east to talk with his publisher.

I didn't learn any more about Uncle Hugh or get to see his room. Mom said Grandfather would talk about him when he was ready. I thought that wouldn't be until next summer, but I was wrong.

That fall I had my class picture taken. The first grade picture had been a disaster. I had squinted and frowned at the camera, refusing to smile because I was missing both upper front teeth. To make things worse, the neighbor's cat had given me ringworm, and they had to shave my head. I knew then that I was the ugliest kid in the world, and that not even Mom and Dad could love anyone that weird-looking. Somehow they did, though they didn't keep the picture.

By second grade, the new teeth were in, my hair had grown out and I finally felt like smiling. The result was a really good picture that Mom said captured my spirit perfectly. I wasn't sure if I wanted my spirit captured, but I liked the picture.

"That can be your Christmas present for Grandfather Kneale and for Grandma and Grandpa Brooks," Mom said.

Mom was acting funny that fall. I didn't know just what was going on, but I knew something was happening. I found out at Thanksgiving dinner.

Grandfather Kneale had come down again, and Mom and Dad had insisted on Grandma and Grandpa Brooks coming over, too. After Grandfather had said grace and we were ready to begin, Mom stood and tapped her water glass with a fork for attention.

"I want you to know that there are seven of us here at the table this year, not six," she said.

I did a quick count. Grandma and Grandpa Brooks, Grandfather Kneale, Mom, Dad, myself. That made six. Where was the seventh?

Mom smiled at me and said, "Jack, next year at this time you will have a baby brother or sister. He or she is growing inside me right now!"

There were smiles all around, and Grandpa Brooks clapped Dad on the back. Grandma asked me what I hoped it would be and I shrugged. I knew where babies came from by then, and I also knew it took close to a year before they were ready to be born. I would be eight before he or she arrived.

"Have you thought of names yet?" Grandma Brooks asked Mom.

"Yes," Mom said. "Martha Ann for a girl, after you and her Grandmother Kneale." I knew Grandma Brooks was Ann, so Grandmother Kneale must have been Martha.

"What if it's another boy?" Grandma Brooks asked.

Mom looked at Grandfather Kneale and said, "If it's alright with you, Dad, I'd like to name him Ehric Hugh. We'll use the Manx spelling, E-h-r-i-c."

Grandfather Kneale looked very solemn. Then he nodded. "I'd be honored," he said. "I think Hugh would be, too." That was all he would say. I think he was happy, but you never could be sure.

On Christmas day we went back to Grandfather's. Mrs. Phelps and Jason were there, and the two stockings hung by the fireplace. After we had gone through them, we exchanged presents. I gave Grandfather my picture, and I remember how he stared at it for a long time. Finally, he set it on the mantle and walked quickly out of the room.

I looked at Mom as if to ask if I'd done something wrong, but she shook her head. "Wait," she said. "I think I know what he's getting."

He came back with another picture and set it on the mantle next to mine. It was a little smaller, not in color, and set in a plain wood frame. It showed a boy about my age. His hair was a little shorter and parted on the other side. Our faces looked enough alike for us to have been brothers. Not quite twins, but brothers.

But this was no brother. It was Uncle Hugh, taken back when he was about my age. How long ago was that? Mom said Hugh died before she was born. How old was he when it happened? How did it happen? There were so many questions I wanted to ask, but I knew it wasn't time yet. Grandfather would talk when he was ready. But when would that be?

"They could be brothers," Grandfather finally said. "Hugh's about a year older there, but look at their faces. When I see Jack, it's like I'm looking at Hugh again. He even sounds a lot like Hugh." He paused and looked at me. "I never had the chance to watch Hugh grow up. Now, maybe I will."

That scared me. Lots of times we get told how we remind someone of somebody we've never known. There's always this hint that goes along with it. Can you try to be even more like that person? I didn't want to be Hugh or anyone else except myself.

Mom sensed my discomfort and talked about it on the way home. "I know it's a little frightening, being asked to measure up to someone you never knew," she said.

"Do you?"

"I felt it all the time I was growing up. It wasn't so bad because I was a girl, but it was there. Your little brother or sister is going to feel it, but it won't be all that hard because you'll be around to help with things. I always felt like I was trying to copy a ghost."

"Why does he never talk about Hugh?"

"Jack, have you ever had a hurt, like a burn or an infection, that was so sore you didn't even want to touch it? And even after it was healing, you were still afraid to touch it, because you remembered how much it hurt when you touched it before?"

"Yeah."

"That can happen with people's lives too. Sometimes things are so painful that even after it's all over, you can't bear to go back to it because you remember how much it hurt when it happened. Did you know your grandfather changed careers after Hugh died?"

"You mean he wasn't always a priest?"

"No. He was a history professor at a university in the same town as the seminary. He came from a wealthy family and had published a couple of textbooks, so he had enough money to quit his job and go back to school. I came along during his first year at the seminary."

Mom had never talked much about when she was a kid. "What do you remember about it?" I asked.

"I can't remember clear back to when I was a baby, but your grandfather says I had colic and cried all night. He used to walk with me up and down the hall and recite his Greek lessons to keep awake. When I started talking, he says I spoke

Classical Greek! Then I got over the colic, so I can't speak Greek any more."

"Did he read The Little Prince to you?"

"Yep. Just like we did for you last year. He's hard to figure out sometimes. Just when you think you understand everything, a whole new part of his personality pops up. But you're good for him. He really looks forward to seeing you each summer."

"I don't do much. I play with Jason and the other kids during the day, and then at night he tells me stories about Spud and the land of Messy Potatoes. I've never asked him about that big book he's writing. I'm too little to understand it anyway."

"Now you are, but someday you won't be," Mom said.

The school year drifted on by. I lost more baby teeth and got permanent ones. I could read chapter books, and I'd grown a couple inches taller.

Mom was growing also, around the middle. By the time school was out, she looked like she had a balloon inside her. She said she felt like she did, too.

I was going to Grandfather's house the last week in June, which was when Martha Ann Brooks was due to arrive. Mom knew by then it would be Martha Ann and not Ehric Hugh. I'm not sure how, but I think there's some test.

Dad was going to drive me, since Mom was too big to fit behind the wheel. But Grandfather said he would come and get me. Mom worried about that, and Dad got worried because she was worrying. But Grandfather Kneale came down anyway.

"I drove a jeep around Iraq for nearly five years," he told Mom after he arrived. "Surely I can manage an American highway."

"It's not that, Dad! It's just. . ."

"It's just that I'm getting old?" he asked. "That's going to happen to all of us, even to Jack." He paused and then added, "Only boys like Hugh stay young forever."

That really surprised me. Grandfather had mentioned Hugh's name before, but only after someone else had brought the subject up. Now he had used his name without being prodded. Something in him was changing.

As we rode back to his house, I noticed that he looked older. He drove slowly and stayed off the freeway, keeping to the old two-lane back roads. "This is how all roads were once," he told me. "Everyone drove slowly. It gave you time to notice things and think about them."

"What are you thinking about now?" I asked because I knew he wanted me to. I still didn't understand him, though there seemed to be a link that allowed me to get a glimpse into his mind now and then.

"I got a letter from my friend Professor Jamal in Iraq," he said. "Things are very bad now, especially for the Kurds in the north. He's afraid they're going to get a lot worse."

"Why?" I asked.

"Iraq is ending its war with Iran. Neither side is strong enough to win. Saddam Hussein is not making his army smaller. He's making it bigger. Professor Jamal wanted to send his son to America to study. I agreed to sponsor him. Instead, the boy was drafted into the Iraqi Army."

"Why would Hussein want more soldiers if he's ending the war?" I asked.

"Why indeed? I think he plans to start another one. The schoolyard bully found someone he couldn't quite whip, so he's looking around for somebody smaller and weaker."

"You called him the bully who runs the school," I said.

"I did, and that's what he is. Remember this about war. The generals and the politicians always get the glory. The poor foot soldiers like Professor Jamal's son get all the misery and pain."

I was quiet for the rest of the trip. Grandfather could tell I was thinking about what he said, and he said nothing more either. I was glad. Some grownups explain and explain and explain as if you were an idiot. Grandfather Kneale knew when to let me figure things out for myself. That was one reason why I loved him.

By the time we reached his house, Grandfather had a surprise for me. "Would you like to stay in Hugh's old room?" he asked as he helped carry my stuff inside. "I think you're big enough now."

I was excited, happy and a little bit scared. Maybe it's silly to believe in ghosts, and anyway, Hugh was my uncle. I still wondered what had happened to him and when?

"Mrs. Phelps and I aired it out for you and got new blankets and bedding," Grandfather said, "but the rest of the room is just as Hugh left it. Nobody has stayed there since he died."

"When did he die?" I asked.

"April, 1956." Grandfather said it slowly, as if he was opening a door in his mind that had been shut for years.

"What happened?"

"An accident. Hugh was riding his bike when a car hit him. It was a hit-and-run. They never found the driver, and there were no witnesses. So we never knew for sure what happened.

"You mean, the driver who killed Uncle Hugh never even got punished for it?"

"Oh, I think he was punished for it," Grandfather said. "He. . . or she. . . has had to live with it for more than thirty years now. Just imagine keeping such a horrible secret penned up inside you, never daring to share it with anyone."

"Yeah, but he should have gone to jail, too!"

"Maybe he did," Grandfather said. "Some people build prisons around their souls and they're locked up there forever."

By then we had reached Hugh's room. Grandfather turned a key in the lock and pushed the door open.

It was like stepping into a museum. There's a smell that takes over places that haven't been used for a long time, and no amount of cleaning can get rid of it completely. The room had a dresser, desk, chair, and bed. There were no posters. "Didn't have them back then," Grandfather explained.

The dresser and closet were empty, but the desk still held some of Hugh's stuff. I picked up a Walt Disney comic book and checked the date on the cover. March, 1956. They cost a dime back then.

"Some of his books are still here. Some are downstairs," Grandfather said. "I can't bear to throw books away. You can take as many as you want back with you."

I didn't recognize any of the authors or titles. They looked like books for someone a year or two older than I was, but I thought I could get through them.

"How old was Uncle Hugh when he died?" I asked.

"One week past his tenth birthday. He was nine in the picture I put next to yours. They're both still on the mantle downstairs."

I saw them again that evening. We both smiled in the same way, as if we wanted to tell the photographer, "Come on! Take the picture! I've got other things to do!" I wondered what other things Hugh was thinking about in the fall of 1955 when he sat and smiled for the camera. What if he had known he had less than a year to live? Would any of us want to know that? I wouldn't.

Grandfather noticed me staring at the pictures and sensed that I wasn't just comparing faces. "We've forgotten these days just how fragile life is, even for children," he said. "In the old times, people had big families because they knew some of their children might die. Now we think we've conquered death for all but the very old. We really haven't. Now and then Nature has to remind us."

"It doesn't seem right, though. It's not fair!"

"The world has never been fair and probably never will be," he told me. "Governments do their best. . . well, most of them do. . . but as long as there are human weaknesses, we will have unfairness, wars, epidemics and famines."

"Then why doesn't God do something about it?"

"God does, but I would have to put you through a course at the seminary to explain it."

"Can't you just give me a hint?"

"All right. Suppose Hugh had not died. Then your mother probably would not have been born, since your grandmother and I decided we would only have one child. And if your mother had not been born, then where would you be?"

"Nowhere, I guess," I said after some thought.

"So Hugh's death gave you a chance to live. The Lord giveth and the Lord taketh away. Remember that your life, and everyone else's too, is a gift from God. Someday you may have power and authority. If you learn nothing else, learn to treat others with fairness and decency. So many people never do."

"Did Spud learn that?" I asked.

"Ah, yes! Spud!" Grandfather said with a sudden smile. "I was wondering when you'd bring him up. Let's see, where did we leave off last time?"

I knew that he knew, but I also knew that he wanted me to tell him. So I said, "He'd just whacked the Viking and knocked him out."

"Of course, the Viking! Tonight I'll tell you more about him and the other things that happened on that day."

Chapter Ten

In which Spud invents a ceremony for taking
a bath and explores an abandoned village
· · · · · · · · · · · · · · · · ·

"His name is Gunnar the Unwashed," Brokenwing reported after the Viking had come to. Spud and Malcolm had bound him securely with rope so the raven could nip him easily. The Viking glared and jabbered in a language that reminded Spud of someone trying to talk while sneezing.

"He's speaking Old Icelandic," the raven added. "Strange language! I never before had a chance to hear it."

"What is he saying?" Spud asked.

"If I understand correctly, he is asking you to take his ax and cut his head off with it!"

"What?" Spud cried. "He's tied up and helpless. That would be murder!"

The raven and the Viking held another conversation. "You have defeated him in battle and brought disgrace upon him," Brokenwing said. "His chief and companions are gone. His Viking honor has been ruined. If you don't want to kill him yourself, he begs you to untie him so that he can swim out to sea and drown."

Spud was a good-natured lad who never wished anybody harm. Besides, a dead Viking was no good to anyone, whereas a live servant could be very useful.

"Ask him if he will accept me as his new chief. Tell him I want him by my side if I have to do battle again."

Brokenwing and Gunnar the Unwashed had another conversation. "He is willing to die for you whenever you wish," the raven reported. "He believes you've been touched by Thor." Spud looked puzzled. "The Old Norse God of Thunder," Brokenwing explained.

"Oh. Ask him if he can do anything besides wield an ax."

"He says he was the ship's cook when he wasn't raiding and pillaging," the raven translated.

"Then that can be his job here!" Spud cried. "Unite him and. . ." He stopped and sniffed. Gunnar the Unwashed was very well-named. Spud knew he himself was no model of cleanliness, but this Viking absolutely reeked. Even Will or Tom at their worst could not come close to him.

"Tell him his first duty as my subject will be to take a bath and wash his clothes," Spud ordered.

The Viking looked shocked. "He says he swore an oath that he would only wash in the blood of his enemies," Brokenwing reported. "Tell him it's time for a new oath." Spud examined his own tunic and britches and made a decision. "We will all wash ourselves in the creek," he said. "Tell him it's a great honor and a special ceremony in this land."

Spud knew Ma had made a fresh batch of soap a week or so before she vanished. He found some in the kitchen and cut three chunks. "Malcolm, untie Gunnar and bring him to the creek. I'll come with you. We're all going to have a bath and wash our duds!"

"Can I bring Puppy, too?" the half-giant begged.

"All right, but keep hold of him. Blossom is grazing over in the meadow, and wolves and cattle aren't exactly friends."

The stream ran salt water and was fairly warm. The day was clear, with the sun directly overhead and the protective fog bank low on the horizon. Spud left his clothes on the bank, leaped into the water and began scrubbing. Malcolm Woolybottom picked up the wolf and jumped to midstream, but even there the water only reached his waist. Brokenwing preened his feathers on the bank.

Gunnar the Unwashed hesitated. Spud wondered why. The Viking was willing to swim out to sea and drown, but not willing to jump into a creek and wash. "Why won't he come in?" Spud asked.

"His vow," the raven said. "He's sure that Thor or Wotan or some other Norse god will strike him down for breaking his word,"

"Then what can we do? Even I can tell he stinks!"

"Get your club. We have to perform a ceremony and release him."

How am I going to do this, Spud wondered as he hiked back to the shed, picked up the nobbeltynook that had knocked the Viking senseless with one blow, and walked back. A ceremony? Spud had never done one. He had never even seen one.

"How do I do this? What do I say?" he asked the raven.

"Latin is good, if you know any."

"Never heard a word of it."

"Then make up something and end the words with *amus*. It will sound enough like Latin to fool him. He's never heard any either."

Spud felt rather silly, but he waved the club over the Viking's head and made up the following verse:

"Washamus, scrubamus, rub-a-dub-dubamus!

Copeamus, hopeamus, don't spare the soapamus!"

He stopped and asked, "How's that?"

"Wonderful!" said Brokenwing. He muttered something in Old Icelandic, then added, "Give him a couple more lines, then whack him one and push him in."

"Hopamus, dropamus, give him a bopamus!

Prideamus, wideamus, you'll have a clean hideamus!"

He rapped the Viking once on the head, and Gunnar the Suddenly Wet tumbled into the creek. Malcolm Woolybottom was so impressed that he insisted the ceremony be done on him, too, so Spud had to repeat the words.

"Now do Puppy!" the half-giant begged.

This is getting ridiculous, Spud thought. But Brokenwing said, "Try it. Another whack might actually tame him."

So Spud spoke the words a third time, gave the wolf a rather smart rap between the ears, and the animal stopped struggling and snarling.

"Bend closer to him," the raven urged. "Don't be afraid!"

Spud did and the wolf licked his face. "See what a simple ceremony can do?" Brokenwing said. "It's all part of being a king."

By the time Spud and his subjects had dried their clothes and themselves, the fog had begun to burn away. Spud knew they were approaching land and wondered idly where and when they were this time. The Kingdom of Messy Potatoes did a quarter-turn widdershins, then bumped into another continent.

Spud ran back to the cottage for his shield. Gunnar's great battle-ax lay next to it. Spud thought, do I trust him with it or not? I guess I have to. A good king has to trust his subjects.

"March at my left side and fight there if need be," he said as he handed Gunnar the ax. Malcolm shall be on my right. Brokenwing shall sit where he pleases and translate.

By the time they reached the border, the fog had disappeared. The stream had been joined to a creek flowing from the new land and now ran fresh and cold. The new land was green and fair to look upon, though Spud had no idea what land it was.

Brokenwing had to explain what had happened for Gunnar the Newly Washed. Malcolm Woolybottom's face was blank, and the wolf growled and cowered between the half-giant's legs. Spud realized they were waiting for him to lead, because that's what a king should do. So he led them across the furrow and into the new land.

He saw cattle grazing in a nearby field and some well-tended farms in the distance. To his left were small hills covered with vines. Spud recognized them as grapes. The creek ran past them through the hills and down to the border and his own stream.

They soon came to a road. Spud saw the tracks of horses and the imprints of cart wheels in dirt that had been softened by recent rains. He saw a signpost a short way ahead and ran to it. There was writing, but Spud could not read what it said. He could barely read in his own language, but he knew enough to realize this was a different tongue.

"Anybody know what it is?" he asked.

Malcolm and Gunnar were stumped, but Brokenwing ruffled his feathers and said, "Spanish."

"What's that?"

"It's the language of Spain, but it's also the language of many lands that Spain held at one time or another. We could be in any one of a great many places," the raven explained.

"Then let's find out. I suppose this sign points to a town?"

"Indeed, it does," Brokenwing said.

"Then let's follow the road and see what we come to. Form up, my merry men. . . and wolf. . . and bird! Forward March!"

The road led toward the vineyard-covered hills. Spud soon saw that they were well-tended, though there was no sign of the people who did the tending.

Spud thought as he marched. Each time his kingdom struck a new land, he gained something. But it never seemed to be what he expected. The Land of the Giants gave him Malcolm Woolybottom. In the Land of Stories he had come away with the wolf instead of the girl. The Vikings had left him the gift of a cook. What was he expected to find here? How would it help him in his quest to find Ma? Was there any meaning to this?

When they reached the hilltop, Spud could see a tiny village in the valley below. It held a dozen houses made from clay and sun-dried brick and two larger buildings. As they drew nearer, they saw that one building had a bell tower and a cross on the door, and the other had a sign over the door showing a cup and a bunch of grapes.

"A church and an inn," Brokenwing said. "We can find everything we need to know in one or the other. Which one should we try first, Your Spudship?"

"The inn," Spud said. "I'm hungry."

But the inn was empty and looked like it had been that way for days. Spud called, "Hey, there! Anybody home?" Gunnar bellowed something in Old Icelandic, and Malcolm rumbled a sentence in his native Giant. None got any response. "Let's try the church," Spud suggested.

The church was vacant, too. They tried all twelve houses. None were locked, but all were empty. No men, women or children. No dogs, cats or chickens. Nothing but a few bugs and a tiny mouse that scurried into a hole as they entered the last house.

"Are they hiding from us?" Spud wondered.

"They're hiding from someone or something," Brokenwing said. "Probably not us, since it looks like everyone has been gone for more than a day. Let's try to find them."

"How? They could be anywhere, and we don't know the land."

"You're forgetting the wolf," Brokenwing reminded him. "He has one of the world's keenest senses of smell and is tame enough to do as Malcolm commands. Tell him what to do, Malcolm."

"Puppy! Find people!" Malcolm ordered, and off they went.

The wolf led them out of the village and back up the hill they had crossed. Suddenly, the wolf veered off the road and plunged into the vineyard. The vines stretched above Spud's head, above Gunnar's, and nearly topped Malcolm Woolybottom's. The path between rows turned, twisted, divided, then divided again. Spud realized they were in a maze. "Keep together!" he ordered.

Suddenly, the wolf stopped, pointed with its nose and growled. Spud pushed his way through a row of vines and found himself in a clearing in the very center of the vineyard. A small group of people huddled together and stared at them as if they were from another world. Spud counted the villagers as they gaped: nine men, eleven women, and six small children.

One man stood out, young and about the age of Spud's brother Tom. The other adults were old enough to be the children's grandparents. There was no sign of any parents.

"How do I talk to them?" Spud wondered.

"Bring one over," Brokenwing said. Spud beckoned to an old man, who approached nervously. "Let me do you first as an example, Your Spudship." Spud grimaced, but held out his arm.

This is what I get for being a leader, he thought. "Ouch!"

"Now set me on that man's arm," the raven said. Spud did and Brokenwing immediately jabbed him. The man cried out and jerked his arm so violently that Brokenwing lost his perch and tumbled to the ground. Gunnar snarled and hefted his ax, but the raven spoke to him in Old Icelandic and he relaxed. Then Brokenwing began to speak Spanish.

The man replied, hesitantly at first, then more willingly. The raven listened, then said something which made the man stop. Spud watched the others while the conversation continued. The elders and small children were quaking with fright. Only the young man seemed more curious than frightened. Finally he approached and held out his arm.

Spud picked Brokenwing up and let him jab the young man's arm. The young man did not flinch. He's brave at least, Spud thought. "What's going on here?" he asked the raven.

"They are hiding from a great war," Brokenwing said. "We are somewhere on the coast of fourteenth-century Spain. The Spaniards and the Moors are getting set to fight a terrible battle, and this village seems to be caught in the middle."

"Which side are they on?" Spud asked.

"It doesn't seem to matter. The Moors think they are for the Spaniards, and the Spaniards think they are for the Moors. If one side wins, they will all be carried off in chains to the dungeons in Valencia. If the other side wins, they will all be carried off in chains to the Alhambra in Grenada."

"Don't seem like much of a choice," Spud admitted.

The young man suddenly spoke up. "He says he's the last young man in the village," Brokenwing translated. "All the others have been taken for soldiers or servants, first by one army, then the other. The elders are hiding him because he is all they have left. He says he is not afraid to fight, but he does not know for what he would be fighting. One side seems as bad as the other. He wants to know which side you are on."

"Tell him neither one, but I might be able to help them," Spud replied. "Ask if they want to stay here and be part of this war or would they like to go someplace else?"

"They want no part of the war," the young man said after the raven translated the offer. "But they cannot leave their homeland. This vineyard and these hills are all they have ever known. Taking them away would be like killing them!"

"Then would you like to go and take your land with you?" Spud asked. Brokenwing translated and the young man looked at Spud, then the old man, then he mumbled something.

"He, uh, wants to know if you have an empty room or two inside your head," the raven said.

Spud made up his mind. This land and these people must be why he came. He wasn't sure what use they would be to him in his quest, but he was sure they were meant to be part of his kingdom.

"Tell the young one to come with us. The others should remain hidden. Tell them there will soon be an earthquake, but they shouldn't worry. It will all be for their good."

Brokenwing translated and this time all the villagers shook their heads in wonder. They were not happy at having the young man leave them, but hard looks from Gunnar, Malcolm, and the wolf stopped any arguments. The Army of Messy Potatoes. . . one boy, one half-giant, one Viking, one wolf and one raven. . . marched with their prisoner back to the border.

Chapter Eleven

*In which Spud outwits two captains and
steals a few miles of the Spanish mainland*
· · · · · · · · · · · · · · · ·

"This will be dangerous," Brokenwing warned as they
led Blossom to the border. "We must work quickly, cover a
great deal of ground *and* make sure we don't accidentally
encircle one of the armies. Then we'd be stuck with them,
and I don't think they would like that!"

"I have a plan," Spud said. "At least, I think I have one."

Spud's plan was to leave Malcolm and Gunnar behind
and take only the village boy with them. "A giant and a Viking marching across Spain might make people suspicious,"
he pointed out.

"And someone plowing a furrow along a highway would
not?" the raven asked.

"They will simply think I'm crazy, so that's what I'll be,"
Spud said. Brokenwing translated for the villager, whose name
was Juan. He was the youngest of three brothers and had been
nicknamed *Juan El Mas Chicito,* Juan the Youngest. Spud
felt a kinship with him because he was also the youngest of
three brothers.

"What happened to your brothers?" he asked through
Brokenwing as they reached the border. Brokenwing translated the reply.

"The Spanish army took one. Then the Moorish army took
the other. Perhaps they are soldiers. Perhaps they are prison-
ers. Perhaps they are both. Who knows?"

"Just like Will and Tom," Spud replied. "You and I both have to look out for ourselves. Now I'm gonna be crazy, and you're gonna be my caretaker."

Spud tied a rope loosely around his neck and handed the end to Juan. "Tell him to hold this like he was in charge of me. If we meet anyone, he's to tell them I'm a harmless lunatic and he's my keeper. He can also say I'm related to someone real important."

He handed Juan a bag of pebbles. "Toss one of these into the furrow behind you every now and then," he said. "When they ask why, you tell 'em I plan to grow a crop of boulders."

Brokenwing translated. Juan smiled and tapped his forehead. *"Es verdad. Muy loco in la cabeza!"* he said.

They had brought a bucket of mud from the enchanted springs. Spud smeared some on the plowshare, stuck the point into the earth and off they went to swipe a few miles of the Spanish mainland out from under the noses of two different armies.

At first they had the road to themselves. Spud began to hope they could make the trip without meeting anyone. But as they neared the signpost, they saw a cloud of dust in the distance. It's either a dust storm nor horsemen, Spud thought as the cloud drew nearer. And I don't feel any wind!

It was, indeed, a troop of cavalry. Juan muttered something, and Brokenwing said, "He says they're Spaniards, probably a scouting patrol for the main army. He wants to know what to do."

"Act like everything is normal," Spud said. "He's only helping a crazy man plow up a roadside. What could be more natural?"

As the soldiers drew nearer, he saw they wore metal breastplates and helmets and carried long lances. Ribbons fluttered from the points. Heavy swords hung at their sides. The horses wore colored padding and big saddles with high cantles in the back. One man wore plumes in his helmet and had shinier armor than the others.

"He's a captain," Brokenwing muttered. "Mind what you say!"

Spud felt an instant dislike for the captain. He was fat in the way some people are when they stuff themselves with their own importance. I'll bet he's a parade-ground soldier and not a real fighting captain, Spud thought. Maybe I can have some fun here.

"Can he understand what you say?" he asked Brokenwing.

"No. Only you and Juan can understand me. I've nipped you and have your blood in my throat. The soldiers will only hear bird cries. Ah! It looks like they're going to stop and question us. Better start being a madman. I hope you're a good actor!"

The captain called out a challenge in Spanish. Juan removed his hat and bowed. "The captain wants to know who we are and what we are doing here," the raven translated.

Spud rolled his eyes, made a face and said, "We are looking for fools, and I think we just found one!"

"I am the keeper of this madman you see here," Brokenwing said in Spanish to Juan, who repeated it to the captain. "He is an idiot, but quite harmless."

"Why is he plowing up the roadside?" the captain asked.

"He is planting pebbles and thinking they will grow to be great boulders. He wants to raise a range of high mountains this year."

"Hey there, Captain!" Spud added. That nose of yours reminds me of a big ol' cucumber! Be careful I don't slice it off and cook it up for supper!"

"What does he say?" the Captain asked Juan.

"Uh, he babbles," Juan said. "I think he means to say you are a great soldier, but you mustn't keep him from his work."

Meanwhile, Spud smiled innocently and added, "Captain, your rear end is so enormous, I'm amazed your horse doesn't break its back." The captain ignored Spud, but glared at Juan the Youngest. "Why are you not marching with us against the Moors?" he asked.

"Because I must protect this poor lunatic," Juan answered. "He is the nephew of the Duke of Bejar, who is too ashamed to house him at his castle, but still wishes to keep him safe from harm."

Spud rolled his eyes again and remarked, "Captain, you smell like a fish that was caught last week and left out in the sun. Be careful when you meet the enemy that the wind blows your scent toward them. Those with good smellers will turn and run!"

"He says that you are a true hero," Juan told the captain. "If you wish, when he is done with the mountains, he will plant some special pebbles and grow you a palace of agate!"

The captain laughed and pointed to Spud's head. "The lantern is there, but the flame has gone out!" he guffawed.

"Is that last night's beer I see on your upper lip?" Spud asked with a wide smile and a gentle voice. "Or do you always blow your nose into your mustache?"

"See what I have to put up with?" Juan said quickly. "Now he offers to plant a chip of marble and grow a statue to celebrate the great victory you will win over the Moors!"

The mention of the hated enemy brought a scowl to the captain's face. "Pah!" he said. "I have no time to waste on *locos!* Go with God, Young Man, and may your poor friend recover his wits someday!"

Spud rolled his eyes again. "And may your britches split across your fat behind the next time you bow to the king!" he said in parting. Brokenwing did not translate any of this.

After the Spaniards had galloped off, Spud smeared more mud on the plowshare and started up the hill to the vineyard where the villagers hid. The cavalry were going in the opposite direction, so they could annex the land without getting the fat captain and his men with it. If they could also avoid the Moors, they might get away cleanly.

They had plowed around the vineyard and the village and were turning back toward the coast when they saw another dust cloud in the distance. "If they're Moors, we're in trouble, unless you or Juan can speak their language," Spud said.

"I know only a few words, which I learned many years ago in Baghdad when I was advisor to the Caliph," Brokenwing replied. "But if they are scouting, they would want to question villagers. So at least one of their party should know Spanish."

"Well, we can't hide. They'd cross our track before we could reach the sea. Then we'd be stuck with them. We'll have to try to send them off in another direction."

"Too late to hide anyway. . . they've seen us! Beware, Your Spudship! Meeting one foolish captain was lucky. To meet with two on the same day would be more luck that anyone could hope for!"

The Moorish patrol rode up at a gallop, fanned out and surrounded Spud, Juan, Brokenwing, and Blossom. They wore less armor than the Spaniards, had fewer ribbons on their lance points and carried curved scimitars instead of broadswords. They looked every bit as deadly as the Spanish patrol.

Their captain was a small man with sharp eyes and a long, thin mustache. He shouted something in a language Spud figured was Arabic, because Juan the Youngest shook his head and replied, "*No comprendo, Señor Capitan.*"

The captain scowled and beckoned to one of his soldiers, who came forward and spoke in a language Spud figured was Spanish. Juan replied and there was a pause as the soldier translated for the captain and Brokenwing translated for Spud.

"He wants to know if the Spaniards are about, and Juan told him yes. Now he wants to know how we escaped them."

Spud was thinking hard. This captain was no fool, and playing crazy would not work with him. What would? How was this captain different from the Spaniard? Suddenly, Spud knew the answer.

"Have Juan tell him the truth," he said. "We acted like I was a lunatic, and the Spaniards believed it and let us go."

Brokenwing translated for Juan, who spoke to the soldier, who translated again for the captain. "What is your idea?" the raven asked as they waited for the reply.

"To get them to forget about us and go after the Spaniards," Spud replied as the Moorish captain spoke again.

"The captain wants to know if you think *he* is foolish enough to believe such a tale," Juan reported.

"Tell him no," Spud said. "Tell him we can see he is a brave man and not at all like the Spaniards said he was."

"He wants to know what you mean by that," Juan reported after Spud's remark had gone through two translations.

"Tell him that a big Spanish captain said all Moors were, uh, puny little worms who wouldn't dare challenge powerful men." As Brokenwing translated for Juan, Spud tried to think of more insults. He sensed this Moorish captain was a fierce, proud man who took insults very seriously.

Juan and the soldier repeated what Spud had said. The Moorish captain's scowl grew deeper, and he clapped a hand to the hilt of his scimitar as he mumbled something in Arabic. It was not translated, but Brokenwing clacked his beak when he heard it and said, "I recognize that expression! If you wanted to make him mad, you've just done a very good job!"

"Tell him the Spaniard said he would skin all of them alive and use their hides for horse blankets if they dared approach his troop, which is just beyond that hill over yonder," Spud added as he pointed in the direction the Spaniards had gone.

The Moor's eyes blazed with fury. He drew his scimitar and shouted a command to his troop. The horsemen dashed off, and Spud put more mud on the plowshare. "I think we'd better finish before the survivors come looking for us," he said. "Whichever side wins, they're not going to be in a very good mood!"

Blossom needed no urging. She had done this often enough to know what was going to happen. The sooner she got it done, the sooner she could go back to grazing in peace. She strained for the border as the sea came in sight. It was all Spud could do to keep control of the plowshare.

By the time they reached the old furrow, Spud figured the Moors had crossed beyond the new one. . . unless the Spaniards had turned to give battle. Somehow he didn't think the fat Spanish captain would be eager for a fight against equal odds. "Here's hoping everybody got clear!" he said and urged Blossom across the line.

This time the earthquake was much more severe. A sharp jolt followed a long rolling rumble and knocked everyone flat as part of the Spanish Coast split off from Europe and floated away with the Kingdom of Messy Potatoes. Spud and Blossom were used to it and got up quickly, but Juan the Youngest lay stunned.

The fog formed quickly around the island's rim. Spud caught one last glimpse of Spain before it vanished and they were alone on the sea again. "Which side wins the battle?" he asked Brokenwing as he picked the raven out of a small ditch.

"It doesn't really matter," Brokenwing replied. "Both sides will say it was the will of God and then go on hating each other as much as ever. We are well clear of it, and so are the villagers. Let's give thanks for that!"

"Let's give thanks to Blossom, too!" Spud added as he unharnessed the cow. He realized she had drawn a plow through strange lands without a moo of complaint, faced hostile soldiers, giants, Vikings, and even wolves and earthquakes. In her own quiet way, she was one of the bravest creatures he had ever known.

He threw his arms around her neck and cried, "Good Old Blossom! We're gonna find Ma someday! She'll be in one of these lands you plow for us! I know it! Then we'll all settle down again!"

Blossom blinked her huge brown eyes, nuzzled him with her nose and then went back to grazing.

Gunnar and Malcolm were amazed by the new land. Malcolm clapped his hands for joy, while Gunnar babbled away in Old Icelandic. "He says you have great magic," Brokenwing translated. "He wonders if you are Thor."

"Naw. Tell him I'm just a poor farm-boy-turned-king of a little old island. Although," he added, "it did get a mite bigger today."

Juan the Youngest slowly got to his feet and looked around in a daze. "Tell him he's safe," Spud urged Brokenwing. "Have him get the villagers and tell 'em there are no more enemies and no more battles! We'll all live together in peace!"

"Don't be too sure of that," Brokenwing cautioned. "You don't know where we're going to wind up next."

The fog had once more settled like a shield around the enlarged Kingdom of Messy Potatoes. The land bobbed gently up and down, but the motion was less noticeable now that the country was so much bigger. They were adrift in time and space and heading who knew where.

Chapter Twelve

In which Spud has a very narrow escape and
shares some stories with his subjects

· · · · · · · · · · · · · · · · ·

The Kingdom of Messy Potatoes had drifted in the fog for more than a week. With the addition of New Spain, the island had more than doubled in size. This meant it no longer bobbed up and down as much, which was fine with Spud. Malcolm Woolybottom tended to get seasick when the ocean was rough.

Spud was worried. They usually sailed only a day or so before striking land again. Now, the ninth day after breaking free from Spain, the fog surrounding them showed no sign of thinning. The weather grew warm and humid. Clouds danced overhead each day, bringing sudden showers and once a thunderstorm so violent that Old Tom dashed in from Hood's Woods where he had been living and hid under Ma's old bed in the cottage.

Spud had just asked Gunnar if he knew where they might be going. The Viking shrugged and said, "The sea-road is wide and runs on forever." Spud was amazed at how quickly Gunnar and Malcolm were learning his language. Daily nips from Brokenwing must be helping. Juan the Youngest and the Spanish children were also fast learners. "Why do you call it the sea-road?" Spud asked.

"To a Viking, the sea is a highway," Gunnar said. "I have traveled much, by water and by land, but never at the same time like this. I marvel tha. . ."

"Listen!" Spud cried. "Did you hear something just now?"

They had reached the stream that once divided Spud's land and were not far from the fog that surrounded the island. The stream was running salt water and was very broad and deep.

"I hear nothing but you and the wind," Gunnar said.

"I'm sure I. . . Yes! There it is again!"

Someone was calling for help. He ran to the bank and stared upstream and downstream. The cry came again, louder this time.

"Help! Help me, please!"

It was a girl's voice, but it couldn't be one of the villagers. They stayed up in the hills of New Spain. Who was she? Where had she come from? Where was she now?

"Help! Save me! Help!"

Something moved at the very edge of the fog curtain. He saw a hand, an arm, then a head, bobbing in midstream. It *was* a girl, struggling against the current sweeping her out to sea!

"Help!" she cried again.

"We're coming!" Spud shouted. "Hurry, Gunnar!"

"I see nothing but the water!" Gunnar cried. I hear nothing but the wind! No one is there!"

"No! She's there and I have to save her!" Spud kicked off his boots, peeled off his tunic and dived into the water. It was warm, but way too deep to touch bottom. A strong current pulled him seaward toward the girl struggling at the edge of the fog.

"Help!"

He could see her clearly now. Her hair was pale yellow and her bare arms white. She was not from the village, but the current was taking her closer and closer to the fog and the open sea beyond!

Gunnar shouted, "Come back!" But Spud paid no attention. He had already reached midstream. The current was carrying him straight toward the girl, who struggled to stay afloat. He could see she was beautiful, but who was she?

A stone flew past his head and splashed directly in front of him. He looked back and saw Malcolm, with Brokenwing on his head, running along the bank. The half-giant stopped and threw another stone. Spud watched it arc over his head and strike the water alongside the struggling girl.

A terrible change came over the beautiful face. The fear in her eyes turned to rage. Her skin changed from white to green. She screamed out her anger and dived. Spud stared in disbelief. From the waist down she was *not* a girl! She was not even human! The lower half of her body was that of a fish!

"Mermaid!" cried Brokenwing. "Swim for the bank or she will draw you out to sea!"

Spud turned and struck out for the bank, but the mermaid called to him from the fog. "Leave this land and come with me! I'll show you the secrets of the sea!" Her voice was soft and pleading. He tried to block it out, but the sound seemed to pull him toward her. "Look at me!" Brokenwing urged. "Remember how we resisted the tempter at Count Rolph's castle!"

Spud fixed his eyes on the raven and forced his arms and legs to drive him toward the bank. The pleading voice grew fainter. Gunnar and Malcolm waded into the stream and reached out to him. As he grasped their hands, the mermaid gave one final wail. Then he was safe on the bank and she was gone.

"Close!" the raven murmured. "A little too close!"

"Who. . .who was she?" Spud gasped.

"More than just a mermaid," Brokenwing replied. "She's one of the tempter's agents. Or one of his victims. Or perhaps both. I fear the tempter wants you badly, Your Spudship. I was a fool to underestimate his power. He can even seek us here."

"Then he'll be back in another disguise?" Spud asked.

"Yes, though we're safe for the time being. We defeated him twice at Count Rolph's castle, once at Grandmother's and now here. Each defeat wounds him, and it takes time for him to recover. Each defeat also makes him more desperate and determined. We will have to deal with him again."

"Was the mermaid like the wolf and the storyteller?" Spud asked. He knew he would never forget that face and that voice.

"Yes. The tempter has power to use good things to work evil deeds. A wolf is not wicked in its natural state. Storytellers are usually nice to have around for everybody. As for mermaids. . . well. . ."

"Do you know much about mermaids?" Spud asked. "Ma never told me anything about them."

"I could tell you some stories. . ." the raven began.

Spud had another idea. His subjects were scattered and kept to themselves. The villagers stayed in the hills of New Spain. Malcolm spent his time training the wolf or plowing. Gunnar the Twice-Washed (because he now washed twice a day) roamed the island's rim looking for fish and acted as the Royal Chef. Something was needed to bring them all together.

"We will hear your stories tonight at the old stump," he said. "If Malcolm or Gunnar or Juan or the villagers have any to share, we will hear them, too. It's a chance for all of us to get to know each other, because we could be stuck here together for a long, long time."

"Excellent idea, Your Spudship!" Brokenwing said. "The fog shows no sign of thinning. We'll be adrift for at least another day. Malcolm can tell Juan to fetch the villagers after supper."

Malcolm and the wolf set off right after the evening meal. Gunnar had made a collar for the former beast, who now trotted by the half-giant's side like a puppy with a master.

They returned just before sunset. Malcolm carried three children on his broad back and one under each arm. The smallest child rode on the wolf. Juan the Youngest managed to keep up with Malcolm by trotting the whole way, but the old villagers lagged far behind.

Spud waited for the stragglers to arrive. Then he stood on the stump and spoke to them.

"We're here tonight to share some stories and learn about each other," he began while Juan translated for the old villagers. "Today I had an adventure with a mermaid. This is what happened."

Spud told his tale as simply as he could. When he finished, he said, "Brokenwing knows something about mermaids too. So now I'd like him to tell you a story."

"Very well," the raven said. "Sometimes men have been known to hunt mermaids because, if you can catch one, she will have to grant you a wish."

A few of the old villagers nodded when Juan translated for them. Apparently, they knew something of mermaids, too.

"One day such a man did catch a mermaid. She promised to grant him a wish if he would let her go. Now, most men would wish for money or power, but this man was different,"

Spud glanced around the group. Everyone listened attentively. No one stirred or made a sound.

"This man loved music above all else," Brokenwing continued. "But he could never master a single instrument. On the flute he was terrible. On the violin he was even worse. On the guitar? Well, we won't even speak of that! No one could stand his playing, not even him.

"This man wished that he might sound better than any other musician who ever played, whatever the instrument. The mermaid said, 'I can grant you that wish. But first I must ask you this. Do you want to sound better to yourself or to others?'

"Since this man loved music even more than his friends, he said, 'To myself, of course.' His wish was immediately granted. From that day on he *thought* he sounded better than any musician who had ever played. He played all day and all night. Everyone else thought he was even worse than before, and no one ever went near him again. Listeners, do you think his wish was a good one, or not?"

"Well," Spud finally said, "it was his wish and he's the one who has to live with it. Reckon you'd have to ask him. Gunnar, do you have a mermaid story you could share?"

"I know many tales, for I was the bard as well as the cook on my ship," the Viking answered. "I recall one I wrote about a mermaid and a young member of our crew. It was a song to be chanted, and it does not rhyme in your native common language."

"Then sing it as you wrote it," Spud said. "Brokenwing can translate for me, and Juan the Youngest will translate again for the villagers."

The Viking jumped onto the stump and began his song. This is how Brokenwing translated it.

"Fast did our dragonship fly o'er the sea-road.
Men at the oars rowed swiftly and strong.
Fair was the wind and bright shown the moonlight.
Treasure was ours and the course set for home.

"Then, as we passed a low-lying island,
Young Eric arose from his bench and his oar.
He was the son of my wife's older sister,
And this his first trip with the Northmen to war.

"'What is it, Young Nephew?' I cried from the stern
As he stared at an island just off the port beam.
'Can't you hear it?' he answered.
'The singing! The singing!
She wants me to come to her home in the sea!'

"'I hear nothing!' I answered and ran quickly to him.
'Beware of the sounds that you hear in the night!'
But he leaped from the prow before I could reach him,
Yet never a splash did I hear or I see!

"'Stern all! Back water!' I cried to the oarsmen.
'He's mad from the moonlight, and we'll save him yet!'
But there was no sign of him in the dark water,
Not even a ripple on the face of the sea!

"Then, as we looked on with eyes unbelieving,
The island dissolved into mist, into fog.
And, as it vanished, I heard the boy singing,
And I knew that the mermaid had chosen her mate."

Gunnar's eyes were full of sadness and longing when he finished his tale. Spud wondered how much of it was true. Gunnar had not seen the mermaid that called to him, nor the one in the story. He wants to see them, Spud realized.

"What does it mean?" he asked the Viking.

"The mermaid sings in a voice that can only be heard by the pure in heart. That's who she wants to lure away," Gunnar explained. "That's why you heard and saw her today, yet I couldn't. I've seen war and battle and shed men's blood. The wicked like me never see her, and we hear her only when she is angry or taunting. You, though, have killed no one. You spared my life, though you could easily have killed me. You even spared the wolf."

"The tempter knows mermaid lore, too," Brokenwing said. "He must have told her about you. We were lucky that Malcolm could see her, as well."

He had saved Malcolm. Now Malcolm had saved him. This gentle half-giant with the sheep's hide on his back could do the work of four men in the field and had tamed the wolf so it followed him around like a puppy. True, he ate enough for four men. But there were plenty of fish in the sea, and potatoes grew thick in the messy old field.

"Malcolm, do you know a story about mermaids?" he asked.

"No," Malcolm said. "Giants don't tell many stories, and they never go down by the sea. The only story I remember is how giants came to be giants."

"Then tell us that one," Spud said. So Malcolm did.

"Long ago everyone was the same size and the same color," the half-giant began. "Some people were not happy with that and wanted to be bigger. They plotted how they could be.

"In those days people slept through the winter like bears. They had big pouches in their stomachs where they stored food for long winter sleep. The food in one pouch made them grow. The food in another made them smart. In another it made their skin and hair and eyes the same color. People had many stomach pouches then.

"Somehow these plotters found out which pouch held food for growing. So they stayed awake until the others had gone to sleep for the winter. Then they cut their stomachs open, took out the growing pouches and kept them for themselves."

Spud wondered how people survived having their stomachs cut open and part of their innards pulled out, but he didn't say anything. It was a good story, true or not.

"In order to make room for extra growing pouches," Malcolm continued, "the plotters had to give up something. But what? There was a pouch for kindness. They didn't want that. They took it out and put it in the sleepers.

"So that is why giants are big and mean and regular people are small and kind. After the people found out what had happened, they stopped going to sleep for the winter. They also blended all their pouches into one big stomach for everything they ate."

"Well done, Malcolm!" Spud cried. Two of the old villagers then told stories, and Brokenwing translated for Spud, Malcolm, and Gunnar. Just as the second tale ended, the raven's voice changed and Brokenwing's last word was, "Quark!" Spud knew that midnight had come.

No one felt like getting jabbed again, so the gathering broke up. Malcolm loaded the small children, who were now all asleep, on his broad, woolly back and returned with the villagers to the hills of New Spain. Juan the Youngest stayed behind to talk with Spud.

"Was it true? You really saw a mermaid?" he asked.

"I sure did. I almost got close enough to touch her."

"What was she like?"

"She was the most beautiful and the most dangerous creature I ever saw!" Spud said. "I was in love and terrified at the same time."

"Let me move down here with you!" Juan begged. "You get to have adventures. You meet mermaids and giants and Vikings. I've never had a real adventure in my life! The only girl I ever liked ran off with a soldier when the last war started.

Maybe I can meet a mermaid or a giant down here. I sure won't meet anything up in those hills!"

"If you'll help with the work, come on down," Spud said.

He now had a half-giant, a Viking, a crippled raven, a wolf and a young Spaniard at his side. Spud's band of followers was growing larger.

Chapter Thirteen

*In which Spud solves the mystery of the portable
giant and pulls off another rescue*
· · · · · · · · · · · · · · · · ·

Spud was shearing Malcolm Woolybottom when he saw
the fog beginning to lift. His kingdom had been adrift for
more than two weeks, and the weather had gone from hot to
cold and back to warm again. This made Malcolm's fleece
grow quickly. An old woman from the village gathered the
wool as Spud sheared. She smiled and jabbered in Spanish.

"She says it's fine wool," Juan the Youngest translated.
"She will spin it and make new clothes for the children. She
hopes it will grow back fast. They need lots of new things."

"See, Malcolm?" Spud said as he clipped the last of the
fleece. "Now all the village children will wear a bit of you
every day." He had found the old clippers in the shed. Ma
had once owned sheep and had taught Spud how to use them,
since Will and Tom were too lazy to learn. Malcolm would
not trust anyone else with them.

The kingdom began to swivel. A series of mild earthquakes
warned Spud they were about to bump into another land. He
and Malcolm were used to it, but Juan's eyes grew wide with
fear and the old woman fell to her knees.

The bump wasn't so bad this time, since there was more
area to absorb the shock. Spud hoped the village was still
standing.

"Call Gunnar and let's find out where we are," he said to
Malcolm Woolybottom, whose bottom and back were now
less woolly.

"Let me come too!" begged Juan the Youngest.

"All right," said Spud. "And Malcolm, bring the wolf."

Spud, Brokenwing, Malcolm, Gunnar, Juan, and the wolf set out to explore the new land. They left Blossom ready to plow in case they needed to make a quick exit.

The new land joined theirs directly across Hood's Woods from New Spain. It would have once been the northeast corner, but Spud couldn't say what direction it was now until he had a chance to watch the sun travel across the sky.

"Let's go!" he said and led his troops across the frontier.

The new land was low and marshy near the border, but grew higher and rockier as they traveled. There were signs of civilization, though they met with no one as they marched. Spud saw fields that seemed to be flooded.

"Any idea where we are?" he asked Brokenwing.

"We must be somewhere in the Orient," the raven answered.

"Where's that?" He glanced at Malcolm, Gunnar, and Juan to see if they knew, but they seemed as puzzled as he was.

"The world is bigger than you can ever dream," Brokenwing said. "We may have come thousands of miles or kilometers or leagues or versts or whichever way you want to measure the distance. And who knows where we may be in time? Perhaps hundreds of years away from last week!"

"I don't feel any older or younger," Spud said.

"But you could be three hundred years old now. Or perhaps it is four hundred years before your great-grandfather was born."

"But why here and why now?" Spud wondered.

They came to a road and followed it inland. Malcolm, with his great height, was the first to see the village ahead. From a distance it looked deserted. Spud sensed there were people there, perhaps hiding, just as the Spaniards had.

"Why is everyone always afraid of us?" he asked Brokenwing.

"Maybe it's not us," the raven said. "Maybe they are threatened by something else. Maybe we have been sent to save them."

"Well, before we can save 'em, we have to find 'em," Spud said as they came to the town. It was larger than the Spanish village, though not by much. It seemed empty, though Spud had the feeling they were being watched.

"See if the wolf can find anybody," he said to Malcolm.

The half-giant slipped the rope from Puppy's collar, and the wolf darted straight for an open doorway. Spud heard growls and a yell of alarm from inside the house. A man ran out with the wolf right behind him, snapping at his heels, and herding him toward Spud and his band.

The man seemed old. His eyes had a different shape, and his skin was darker yet lightly yellow.

"As I thought, we are in the Orient," Brokenwing said.

"You mean this guy's an Orient? Never heard of such a thing!"

"No. 'Orient' is a word that means 'East'. . . the eastern part of the world. This could be any of a great many countries."

"Then let's find out which one it is," Spud decided. "Gunnar, present arm!"

The Viking held out an arm for the raven to jab. Spud was thankful he now had followers to do some of the more disagreeable jobs. The strange man watched as the bird stabbed its beak into Gunnar's arm. Spud made a sign to the stranger to hold his arm out. Reluctantly, the man obeyed, and Brokenwing stuck him, too.

"Ai!" the man cried. He spoke rapidly in a language that none but the bird could understand. Yet it was strangely pleasing to listen to, even though the rhythm was completely different. He waited for Brokenwing's translation.

"He wants to know if you've been sent by the wicked giant to spy on them," the raven reported. "He begs you to go back and tell him they have already sent the sacrifice."

"What sacrifice?" Spud demanded. "What giant? Does he mean Malcolm?" Spud could feel his anger rising. He did not like being spoken to in riddles.

Brokenwing said something and the man's expression changed from fear to hope and then to joy. He jabbered a long reply that would have been even longer if Brokenwing hadn't stopped him with a loud command that Spud guessed was an order to be quiet.

"He asks a thousand pardons for thinking we were servants of the evil giant," Brokenwing reported. "He meant no offense to Malcolm either. He is glad that we have come and hopes we will speedily slay this evil giant and save the daughter of the honorable Han Lo and the other hostages."

"You mean, he thinks we're in the giant-killing business?"

"He does, indeed!" Brokenwing replied. "You asked a short while ago why we came to this place and time. This may be the answer."

"You boys game enough to take on a giant?" Spud asked the group. Gunnar smiled and hefted his ax. Juan the Youngest swallowed hard and then nodded. Malcolm thought for a moment and said, "As long as it is not one of my relatives." The wolf had no comment.

"Right!" Spud said. "Ask him which way the giant went and where he lives, and we'll be on our way!"

The man replied by pointing to mountains a few miles beyond the village and making a long speech that Brokenwing finally cut off with another command. "It's not far, but you must squeeze through the crack in The Great Cliff That Cannot Be Climbed to get at him," he said. "He doubts if Malcolm or Gunnar will fit."

"Guess we'll find that out when we get there," Spud said and marched his troops off in the direction to which the villager had pointed.

When they reached the mountains, they discovered The Great Cliff That Cannot Be Climbed was very well-named. It was as smooth as glass and rose straight up for several hundred feet. It also stretched away in an unbroken line for as far as anyone could see in any direction. How do we get past this? Spud wondered.

"He said there was a crack. Let's find it," Brokenwing said.

The earth was too hard for tracks, but Puppy picked up a scent which they followed along the base of the cliff until they found the opening. The crack in the rock would be a tight fit for Spud. Juan the Youngest just might make it. But there was no way for Gunnar or Malcolm to squeeze through it.

"Going to have to be just the two of us," Spud told Juan. "You still game?"

Juan swallowed twice and shivered. Then he nodded and said, "If you go, I will come with you."

"Take Puppy, too!" Malcolm offered.

Spud took off his pack, turned sideways and began inching his way through the crack in the cliff, pulling his shield behind him. At one point the rock rubbed against his stomach and back at the same time. Juan, who was just a mite bigger, was going to lose some hide.

Something's wrong here, Spud thought as he squirmed and squeezed his way through. It's a tight fit for me, almost impossible for Juan and the wolf, and completely impossible for Malcolm or Gunnar. So how does a giant even bigger than Malcolm do it?

Spud could see light ahead and guessed the passage width was twenty to thirty feet. It had just enough of a bend to prevent anyone seeing from one end to the other. Behind he could hear Juan struggling through the narrow spot. Sure hope you don't get stuck, he thought.

As if in answer, Juan cried, "Spud! Help! I'm wedged tight!"

Spud couldn't reach Juan with his hand, so he unhooked the nobbeltynook from his belt and held it out. "Grab on and I'll pull!" he said.

Juan grabbed, Spud pulled, and Juan popped free. Powerful magic in this little club, Spud thought. They made their way through the rest of the passage and out into a strange new land.

Spud saw right away that it was good land, just untended. There were no signs of crops or plowing. Weeds, brambles, and bushes grew everywhere. Brokenwing looked about from his perch on Spud's shoulder and clacked his beak.

"It looks like a giant lives here," he said. "They never work the land, and they won't allow anyone around them to work it."

"Then how do they eat?" Spud asked.

"That is not a pleasant topic," Brokenwing replied. "They rob, steal and force others to pay them tribute."

"Like those villagers back there?"

"Yes. The giant will take and take until they have nothing left. Then he will destroy them and move somewhere else."

"Not if we can stop him!" Spud said grimly.

The wolf found a path through the bushes and brambles. As they marched along, Spud considered a vital problem. "Uh, how *do* you fight a giant?" he asked as quietly as he could.

"It depends upon the type of giant you face," the raven said. "Most are blustery cowards at heart, so your best chance is to be bold and fearless."

"That's fine. . . as long as we ain't dealing with a bold, fearless giant!"

"I don't think we are," Brokenwing said. "I get the feeling that this giant thrives on the fear he plants in others."

"We'll soon find out," Spud said. "That's him up ahead!"

The giant suddenly loomed up before them. He was more than twice the size of Malcolm Woolybottom. A huge hat with a wide brim covered his face. Slowly he raised one arm as if ordering them to halt. Then he spoke in a language that sounded familiar.

"He says he will tear us to pieces if we do not turn and flee," Brokenwing translated.

"Is he speaking the language of the village?" Spud asked. "That's strange! I thought giants had a language all their own."

"It is odd," the raven admitted. "Maybe he's a bilingual giant and thinks we're from the village."

"Then it's time he learned we're not! Tell him we've come to run him off or kill him! It's his choice."

"He won't understand unless I nip him first."

"Then we won't bother with words!" Spud slipped the shield on his arm and brandished the nobbeltynook. He actually felt more like running than fighting, but he knew he couldn't outrun someone with legs that long. Maybe a bluff would work.

Then help came from an unexpected source.

The wolf had slunk off through the brush at the first sight of the giant. Spud thought it was running back to Malcolm. Instead, Puppy sprang out of the brush behind the giant and bit him on the back of one huge leg!

The giant didn't react. He didn't even seem to feel the bite. But Spud heard a sound. . .fssss! . . . like air escaping, and the huge leg began to shrivel. Was this nothing more than a huge scarecrow? Spud closed in and whacked the shriveled leg as hard as he could.

Crack! Something snapped and the giant began to topple. Slowly at first, then faster and faster! Spud expected to feel the ground shake when the giant hit, but he felt nothing and heard only the faintest of thumps. The sound of escaping air grew louder, and the giant's whole body began to collapse!

A small voice began crying from somewhere inside the framework. "He says he's trapped and can't get out," Brokenwing reported. "He's begging you for help!"

This, Spud decided, was the strangest fight he had ever been in. The giant's body was nothing more than a collection of skins and hides sewn over a wooden frame and pumped up with air. Who was making all that racket inside? Spud drew his knife, cut open the skin, and pulled out a little old man.

"Who are you?" he demanded. Then he realized he needed Brokenwing to get an answer. He grabbed the little man and held him until the raven took a nip.

"Who are you?" he demanded again. Brokenwing translated the question, and the little old man began to babble.

"His name is Yin Fang." the raven said. "He begs you not to kill him. He has never done anything really bad. He only took the giant's place two years ago."

"Tell him to explain what he means and be quick about it. I ain't in the mood to listen to riddles right now!"

Yin Fang spoke rapidly for a long time. Finally, Brokenwing shut him up with the same command he had used earlier on the villager.

"Apparently, a real giant lived here not so long ago," the raven reported. "He was wicked and terrorized the countryside for years. The people had to give him tribute from their fields, their herds, and even their children and young people. Yin Fang was one of those sent as a sacrifice."

"Then why is he still alive?"

"He was clever with his hands and a good talker," the raven replied. "He made things for the giant and kept him entertained. So the giant let him live, and Yin Fang became his servant."

"But where is the real giant?" asked Juan.

"He finally died of old age. Yin Fang buried him."

"That must have been quite a job!" Spud commented.

"Then Yin Fang decided to become the giant," the raven said.

"Why?" Juan asked again.

"Because he'd led an easy life for so many years and didn't want it to end. He made a frame, covered it with skins and the giant's clothes, got inside and used a bellows to pump it up and keep himself supplied with air. He walked on stilts inside it and controlled the arms with strings, like a puppet master. He could haul it through the passage at night, blow it up before dawn, then let it deflate and haul it back."

"Couldn't the villagers tell the difference?" Juan asked.

"They were too frightened to come that close," Brokenwing answered after questioning Yin Fang. "All he had to do was show himself for a few minutes at dawn and the people would run away to gather the sacrifice. By the time they came back, he was safe on the other side. He could return and pull the young people through, because they were left tied up and couldn't get away."

"But how did the real giant get past that cliff?" Spud asked.

The raven again spoke with Yin Fang and said, "Apparently, he climbed up on this side. . .it's not so steep over here. . .then climbed down a rope he kept fastened at the top. When he'd done his terrorizing, he climbed up the rope and pulled it up after him."

Spud glared at the cowering little man. "You let this giant rob and kill your own people!" he shouted. "You even helped him!"

"What could I do?" Yin Fang replied as Brokenwing translated. "He would have killed me if I refused!"

"But you kept on taking after the giant was dead!" Spud shouted. "You even took their children!"

"But I didn't kill them!" Yin Fang protested. The daughter of Han Lo and the others are safe in the giant's dungeon. I never harmed them! I just couldn't let them go! They'd tell the others!"

"Then we'll let them go now," Spud said.

They marched Yin Fang back to the giant's huge stone house and made him unlock the dungeon in the cellar. Juan the Youngest went in and led several people out. One was a beautiful girl who leaned on his arm and gazed at him in wonder. We probably look as strange to them as they do to us, Spud realized.

"I'll bet this is the daughter of Han Lo," Juan said. "Isn't she beautiful?" It was plain that he'd forgotten all about the girl who had run off with the soldier.

"What do you want to do with Yin Fang?" Brokenwing asked.

"Lots of things, and none of 'em nice!" Spud answered. "But let's put him in the dungeon and let the villagers decide later."

Great was the rejoicing when Spud and Juan returned and announced the giant was dead. It was even greater when the young people given up for dead returned to their families.

Spud told the story while Brokenwing translated to the old man, who repeated it to the villagers. Spud stuck close to the truth. When he saw how the daughter of Han Lo gazed at Juan, he changed the script a bit and made Juan the hero who had brought down the giant. Brokenwing clacked his beak in approval.

When they heard of the magical island, many younger villagers, and even a few older ones, asked if they could come with Spud. The matter was referred to Han Lo, who made this decision.

"Our village and people have been saved. There is new land for us on the other side of the cliff. Let those who wish to remain go there and build a new life. Let those who wish to go with King Spud take this village with them."

About half the village chose to go with Spud. Two days were spent in moving and saying goodbyes. Then Spud hitched Blossom to the plow and began to cut a new furrow. The Orient would soon be just a little smaller.

Chapter Fourteen

In which a sister arrives, a grandfather gets ready
to leave and a story waits for an ending
. . . .

I stayed ten days with Grandfather Kneale that summer. On the fifth Dad called to say that Martha Ann had been born and weighed seven pounds, eight ounces. I never understood why grownups make such a big deal over how many ounces a baby weighs.

Dad offered to come get us that night, but Grandfather said we would wait till Mom was back home and ready for us. "Your sister is probably going to be around for the rest of your life," he told me. "Let's give her and your mother a little time to get used to each other."

So we drove back the day after Spud plowed away part of China. Or it might have been Korea, Japan, Vietnam or Malaysia. Grandfather said to look at the globe and decide for myself. I picked China because it looked big enough that losing a little piece of its coast wouldn't hurt it much.

We took the old highways again. Grandfather never said much while he drove, but I could tell he was thinking. So I sat and thought, too. I thought about my new sister, just starting her life, and about the man beside me, coming to the end of his. I don't know how I knew that, but I did.

I heard Martha Ann before I saw her. She was yowling when we came through the door. "Just like her mother!" Grandfather said. "She's a Kneale, all right!"

She was all wrapped up in a bundle, the way I had been in that picture. She was bald, cross-eyed and, to me at least, ugly. Mom saw my questioning stare and smiled. "Just wait," she promised. "In a month she'll be the prettiest little girl you ever saw!"

I wasn't so sure of that, but I knew better than to argue.

It took a while, but she did get better. I was given a new title. . . Big Boy of the Family. . . which meant I had to do things while she got all the attention. I couldn't even boss her around.

I really looked forward to school that fall. I was very good at reading, okay at the other things and tough enough to hold my own on the playground. And having a new baby sister did make me a kind of celebrity for a while.

Grandfather came down again for Thanksgiving. He suddenly looked a lot thinner and older. I mean, Martha Ann had changed a lot too. But when you see someone every day, you hardly notice it. I hadn't seen Grandfather in more than four months, and the change in him was scary.

Of course, Mom made a big fuss and tried to get him to eat more than he wanted. He just gave her that thin, dry smile of his and said he knew how much he needed.

Later that afternoon we went down to St. Barnabus Episcopal Church, and Grandfather baptized Martha Ann. He brought along the vestments that made him look like a king without a crown, and our rector let him conduct the service. When he splashed the water over a sleeping Martha Ann, she woke up with a howl of rage and cried for more than ten minutes.

It must have been that long because she was still screaming when they took the picture. It was just like the one they'd taken at my baptism, except my sister was now the baby in the bundle, and I was standing where Grandmother Kneale previously had stood.

I didn't think we'd go back to Grandfather's again for Christmas Day, but he insisted we all come. "It will be Martha Ann's first Christmas, and it may well be my last," he said when Mom tried to persuade him to come to our place instead. "Let her have at least one Christmas at her grandfather's, even if she won't remember it. I have a bunch of things for

Jack, too, and I don't want to lug them down. Better you should do the work than me."

So we made the trip on Christmas Morning, 1988. It had snowed on and off for three days, which was unusual for our part of the country, and even the freeway was slow going. I looked at the dirty snow the plows had heaped along the shoulders and imagined what Grandfather's back roads must be like. I was glad he wouldn't be trying to drive them.

"Would you look at that!" Mom cried when we pulled up in his driveway. "He's put up outside lights!"

He had and they were still on, even though the sun had been up for three hours. Mrs. Phelps was out on the porch to greet us before Dad had the ignition turned off. "Come in before you freeze!" she called out as we unloaded presents and (for once) a peacefully sleeping baby.

"Where's Grandfather?" I asked as I leaped up the steps.

"He's inside, Jack," she said. "He's not strong enough to come out in weather like this."

Grandfather sat in the den in his favorite chair. He looked paler and weaker than he had at Thanksgiving. I knew something was seriously wrong, but I also knew it was useless to ask about it. He would tell you what he felt you should know, when he felt you should know it, and trying to push him was hopeless.

His smile was very real. I knew he was glad to see us. His smiles were always special because he didn't use them often.

"What do you think of the lights?" he asked after we had wished him a Merry Christmas.

"I've never seen the house fixed up like this before," Mom said. "How did you do it?"

"All I did was buy the stuff. Mrs. Phelps and a couple of my former students did all the hard work," he said. "Haven't put up outside lights since 1955. Make sure the baby sees them after it gets dark." I realized that 1955 was the last Christmas Uncle Hugh was alive. It was like he was telling us that this one would be his last.

In addition to the stockings, he had a big tree covered with lights and a pile of presents beneath it. There were gifts for Mom and Dad, for Mrs. Phelps and Jason, but most were for Martha Ann and me.

"I tutor a couple of students who are wonderful people, but hopeless at Old Testament History," he explained. "I got them through the course, and in return they've been my slaves for the past week. The poor creatures spent hours wrapping packages, setting things up and driving me around. I only gave them their freedom three days ago."

After all the presents were opened, an uncomfortable silence settled on the room. Finally, Mom said, "Dad, don't you think it's time we talked this over?" Grandfather nodded. Mom made a motion for me to leave, but Grandfather shook his head.

"No," he said. "Jack's big enough to hear what's going on. Let him stay." He looked at Mom, then at me and said, "I have cancer, Jack. I've been fighting it since I came back from Iraq, but there's nothing left to fight with anymore."

I just nodded. There was nothing anyone could say. I had known it without realizing since last summer in the car.

"I didn't tell you earlier because I didn't want Jack to be afraid. Some people still think it's a disease you can catch."

"I know it isn't," I said. "But how did you get it?"

"I stayed with the Kurds in Northern Iraq. Many of them have died from it. Hussein has it in for them. He might have done something to the water or the air as an experiment before he tried it on Iran."

I remembered how Grandfather had described Saddam Hussein. . . the bully who ran the school. Was Grandfather dying because of him?

Again he seemed to read my thoughts. "It might not have been him at all," he said. "It might have nothing to do with Iraq at all. The point is, I have it and there's no way to get rid of it."

"How long do they give you?" Mom asked.

"They say six months, but I may surprise them. I'm a tough old bird." He looked at me with another thin smile. "Just like Brokenwing," he added.

"What do you plan to do?"

"I've finished the book. The seminary is loaning me a student to help with details and corrections. Mrs. Phelps is going to move in and take care of the place and me."

"Dad!" Mom began. "I can come up and. . ."

"No!" he replied. "You have a new baby. Give your time to her. There's always the phone. But Jack, we still have some unfinished business to deal with."

"You mean the story of Spud?" I asked.

"Yes. I've been writing down the episodes you like. I showed some to my editor, and he says they'd make a good book. Do you think you could help me finish it?"

"When?" I asked.

"I'm afraid we can't wait for summer this time. Do you think you could spare me a few weekends this winter?"

I could tell Mom was uncomfortable with the idea, but there was no way she could refuse. She loved Grandfather too much to turn him down. And I knew that I couldn't. . .and wouldn't. . .say no to him either.

So, on the first clear weekend in January, Dad drove me back to Grandfather's house. Mrs. Phelps had fixed a bedroom for him just off the den because he was too weak to handle the stairs. After dinner he would sit in his favorite chair and I'd pull up another and we talked together, man to man.

"There's something I have to tell you about Hugh," he said that first night in January. "It's been more than thirty years, and I've never been able to share it with anyone. Our last parting was a bad one. We never said goodbye."

"What do you mean?" I asked.

"We got in a fight over something. I can't remember what it was, which means it was nothing important. Hugh was proud and so was I, back then. Neither of us would back down. We each wanted to, but waited for the other to make the first move. Finally, I yelled something at him and he stormed out of the house. Do you know what his last words to me were?"

I just shook my head. There was nothing I could say.

"He said, 'I hate you when you yell like that!' Then he slammed the door and I never saw him alive again. He took off on his bike, probably just looking for a place to cool off. Maybe the accident was his fault. Maybe it was the driver's fault. Maybe it was nobody's fault. He left me with ugly words and the slam of a door. Ten minutes later I heard the sirens."

I stayed quiet, waiting for him to continue.

"I was a history professor when it happened. I quit and went back to school to become a priest. I needed to find an answer why Hugh died that way. I thought I could find it in the Bible or the books of the Church. Well, I did find an answer, but it wasn't in any books."

"Where was it?" I asked.

"It was in your mother, then in you, and now in your sister. Hugh gave up his place in this world so that you could all have yours. I'm telling you this because it will soon be time for me to give up my place. Remember that your life is a loan from God. You can use it however you want, but someday, sooner or later, you have to pay it back."

"Will you get to see your book come out?" I asked. He smiled his thin smile and shook his head.

"It will be at least a year or two before it's done. I have maybe a few months left."

"It doesn't seem fair!" I said. "You won't get to see it after all the work you did!"

"But you will," he said. "It's pretty advanced, so you won't get anything out of it for another ten years or so. It will still be here in ten years, if you want to try."

"Do you think lots of people will read it?" I asked.

"It's never going to be a best seller," he said with a shake of his head. "The publisher won't make very much on it. But that's not what's important."

"Then what is important?"

"People who want that information will have a place to get it. So what if it will only be dozens or hundreds instead of thousands or millions. I've done something to help people, and that's what is good."

"And that's why you want to make a book out of Spud's stories too?" I asked him.

"I suppose so," he said. "You liked them. Others may, too. Stories are like lives. Sooner or later they have to come to an end. I would have liked to string you along for another two or three years, but that won't be possible now. I'm going to need your help with the ending."

"What do you want me to do?"

"Tell me what else you think needs to be told. If this were a book, what more would it need?"

I sat and thought for a long while. Grandfather Kneale was quiet too. He knew when to talk, and when to keep quiet and let you think. He wasn't like some people, who want to start a timer running on you every time they ask a question.

"There has to be one last battle," I said at last.

"You mean, with the tempter?"

"Yes. Because Spud can't just keep dodging him and then getting away. Dad says you can never win backing up."

"There's a lot of truth in that," Grandfather said.

"And somehow it all has to make sense. I mean, there has to be a reason why things happen like they do."

"Fair enough," Grandfather said. "Let's see if we can do it."

And this is what we came up with during the winter and spring of 1989.

Chapter Fifteen

In which Spud conducts a wedding, explores a strange new land, and has an odd encounter with a fish
· · · · · · · · · · · · · · · · ·

A week after annexing a small part of China, King Spud found himself on the stump with a blue botheration on his hands. His kingdom still floated through space and time in a fog bank.

The botheration was that Juan the Youngest wanted to marry the daughter of Han Lo. The daughter of Han Lo wanted to marry Juan the Youngest. Both sets of parents approved. But who would perform the marriage and what kind of ceremony would it be?

The Spanish village had a church, though no priest. "The Moors came and took him away, put a mullah in his place and told us we were all Muslims," an old villager explained while Juan translated. "Then the Spaniards came, took away the mullah, put in another priest and said we were all Catholics again. Then the Moors came back, took away the priest and made us all Muslims again. We just got used to that when the Spaniards came back again."

"That would get confusing after a while," Spud agreed.

"It kept going on until all the priests and all the mullahs refused to come to our village. Now we don't know what we are or what we should believe. What are we going to do about the wedding? What are *you* going to do?"

"Me?" Spud asked. "Hey, do you expect *me* to solve this problem?"

"Of course," said the elder. "You are the king, after all."

"Can I marry them? Is it. . . legal?" Spud asked Brokenwing.

"It's your country and you make the laws," the raven said.

"Then I'll make a law that the king shall have the power to perform weddings until we find someone who can do a better job," Spud decided. "Brokenwing, what *kind* of wedding?"

That was the botheration. Juan the Youngest was either a Catholic or a Muslim, depending on whether a priest or a mullah had been in the village last. The villagers weren't sure. The daughter of Han Lo and her family followed the teachings of someone called Confucius. Spud had never heard of him.

Gunnar and Malcolm were no help. The Viking believed in several Norse gods that no one else had heard of, and Malcolm said giants only believed in being giants.

Spud wasn't even sure what he believed in. Ma had sometimes bowed her head and mumbled things she called prayers, but she never got around to teaching him any. That was probably because Will and Tom always laughed at them.

Spud was going to have to make his own ceremony. . .

The water from the springs always seemed to help. Spud drank some, washed his face, and had an inspiration.

"Have everyone meet tomorrow at the church in the Spanish village," he told Brokenwing. "I want everyone washed and wearing their best. I'll give Malcolm Woolybottom another trim."

The entire population of Messy Potatoes came to the wedding the next day. The Chinese and Gunnar sat on one side of the church, the Spaniards and Malcolm on the other. Spud stood at the front, wearing clean clothes for once, and looking as nervous as the bride and groom.

Brokenwing had told him a lot about weddings and how different cultures celebrated them, but Spud still wasn't sure if he should be doing this. He was the king, after all. If it was going to get done, he would have to do it. He cleared his throat and began.

"Folks, loyal subjects and whatever, we're gathered here today to have a wedding. Here's the bride and here's the groom. They love each other and want to get married. Now if anyone objects to this, let him say so now, and Gunnar here will take him outside and teach him better manners!"

Nobody said a word.

"Good!" Spud continued as an elder from each village translated the service into Spanish and Chinese. "Now then," he said to the daughter of Han Lo, "take a good look at that fellow there beside you." The daughter of Han Lo looked keenly.

"It's easy for you to love him now, because he's all cleaned up and smells nice and is using his best manners. *But*, will you love him when he's worked in the field for a week without changing his shirt, and comes into the house smelling like an old horse and forgets to wipe his boots and tracks mud and maybe even worse stuff all over your clean floor? Will you love him even when he's grumpy and grouchy and his socks smell like two goats have been sleeping in them?"

"Yes, I will!" said the daughter of Han Lo.

"Now it's your turn," Spud said to Juan the Youngest. "Do you see how beautiful this girl beside you looks now? Well, try and picture her after she's stayed up all night with a sick kid, and she's not feeling so hot herself, and her eyes are all red and puffy, and her nose runs, and she coughs in your face and tells you to get your own breakfast because she's going back to sleep. Will you love her as much then as you do now?"

"Yes, I will!" said Juan the Youngest.

"Then either you're both totally crazy or else you're really in love. Will you both promise me as your king that you'll bring your kids up to be useful subjects and not to be lazy and do stupid things like my brothers did?"

"We will!" they both answered.

"Then by my authority as your rightful king and all that, I say you are married now and forever or at least until you're dead, and may God have mercy on your souls!"

"Uh, Your Spudship," Brokenwing interrupted. "That last line is usually said by judges when they sentence someone to death."

"Well, I just sentenced them to love each other until they're dead, didn't I? That's pretty much the same thing."

"Perhaps it is," Brokenwing admitted.

So that was how Juan the Youngest married the daughter of Han Lo, and the whole kingdom rejoiced. But not for long.

The people were just leaving the church when Spud looked at the horizon and saw the fog lifting rapidly. The kingdom was about due for another collision. "Everyone back to your villages!" Spud ordered. "Malcolm, Gunnar, and Brokenwing come with me! Bring the wolf too!"

"What about us?" asked Juan the Youngest.

"We will come too," said the daughter of Han Lo.

"All right, but it's a mighty odd way to spend a honeymoon!" Spud said. "Head up that hill. It's the highest in New Spain. We can see where and what we're gonna hit."

By the time they reached the summit, the fog had nearly cleared. To the right and behind them was ocean. To the left, across Hood's Woods, lay the flat plain of New China. Straight ahead, across Spud's original kingdom, loomed the new land.

"Brace yourselves!" Spud warned. "We're gonna hit!"

The collision came with a low, rolling rumble. The ground beneath them trembled and vibrated. Then came one or two aftershocks. Then everything was quiet again.

"Come on," Spud said. "Let's see what land we're part of now." He led his army down the hill and across the plain, through his original land and on to the new border.

The land was almost treeless but very green. The temperature was mild. A small brook came down from low hills and joined his own stream. Once again there were no signs of people, though Spud was sure that a land like this must have a human population somewhere. Maybe it's good that we don't whack into cities, he thought as he looked over the land. We would probably cause a panic or maybe even a war.

They stopped at Spud's cottage for his shield and nobbeltynook and Gunnar's battle-ax. Spud again set

Brokenwing on his shoulder and stepped across the furrow into the new country.

"Any idea where we are?" he asked the bird.

"Not in the Tropics, not in the Arctic," Brokenwing answered. "Britain, Ireland, America, Russia, perhaps. Maybe Australia, New Zealand, or Argentina."

"Don't believe I've ever heard of any of 'em," Spud said.

"That's because most haven't been discovered yet," the raven replied. "They're still there, and we may be a part of one now. It's a very big world, Your Spudship."

They searched the new land for signs of people or anything else that might give them a clue as to where and when they were. They soon came to a path that must have been made by men. They followed it and soon began to see strange sights.

First they came to a hill. One side had been cut away, and three huge heads had been carved, one on top of the other, into the bare rock. A stream, probably the same one that now flowed into Spud's land, came down from a larger hill and into the topmost head. It gushed out from three openings in the mouth and fell into the second head, where it came out in one stream from the nose. Then it flowed into the top of the third head and came out in a single stream from the mouth. From there it made its way to Spud's land and on to the sea.

"Is that supposed to mean something?" Spud asked.

"It does," said Brokenwing. "Look first at the top head. See how much smaller it is than the others?"

"Yeah, I can see that. What about it?"

"One stream falls in and three flow out," said the raven. "It represents the highest and best kind of men. . . those who give much even though they receive little. They are the rarest. The bigger head below it stands for the worst. . . those who receive much and give little. They are not so rare. The biggest head at the base of the cliff. . . that's the great majority of men. They will give as much as they receive, but no more than that."

"Who'd spend so much time carving such a thing?"

"That I don't know," said the raven. "It was meant as a warning for those who pass by."

"Look up ahead," said Gunnar. "What is that boy doing?"

Spud saw a boy dragging a large branch up to a fire that burned brightly in a meadow just beyond the road. After much effort he managed to lift the branch and throw it on the fire. Then he disappeared into a stand of trees while the fire blazed up. Then a man, dressed in the same clothes as the boy, came out dragging another branch.

"Is that a boy and his father or is this some kind of magic?" Spud asked.

"Watch!" the raven said.

By the time the man got his branch to the fire, the boy's branch had burned and the fire was low. The man heaved his own branch on the fire and walked back into the trees. Soon an old man, dressed the same way, came back dragging a third branch. By the time he reached the fire, the second branch was almost gone. The old man threw the third branch on the fire, walked back among the trees, and the fire burned itself out and the whole scene vanished.

"What am I supposed to learn from that?" Spud asked.

"That poor man stands for those who work all their lives for others. They work hard, but never get to warm themselves at the fire. You may someday be a king over many, Your Spudship. Let your subjects warm themselves at the fire, if they are the ones who tend it."

Spud was still pondering this when Malcolm pointed to yet another strange sight. Two men were thatching a house with what looked like feathers. They finished about half the job, then set out to gather more feathers. Before they could return, the wind blew up and scattered their work, so they had to begin all over again.

"Those two sorta looked like Will and Tom," Spud remarked.

"Indeed, they should," said Brokenwing. "They stand for those who rush out to seek their fortunes with no thought or plan of how they'll do it. By the time they return with anything, what they have is gone and they must begin again.

The farther they traveled into this new land, the more uneasy Spud became. He could see no signs of danger, yet something was wrong. He glanced at Malcolm, Gunnar, and Juan and saw they were nervous too. Even the wolf stayed close by Malcolm with its hackles raised in fear. It was the daughter of Han Lo who figured it out.

"Listen!" she said. "What do you hear?"

"Nothing," Spud replied after listening for a moment.

"That is what's wrong!" she said. "There is no sound but that of our own voices. None of the people we saw made a sound. I can't hear any birds. There is no sound to the wind. That waterfall back there is silent. Even our feet make no sound when we walk!"

To prove her point, she stamped the ground with her foot. There was no sound, even though she stamped hard enough to raise dust. As he stared at her feet, Spud saw that she cast no shadow, yet the day was bright with sunshine. He looked around. None of his band cast shadows. Something was very, very wrong here!

"This place gives me the galloping creepies!" he said to Brokenwing. "I'd like to get out, but aren't we supposed to find someone or something first?"

"Speak up! I can't hear you," the raven said.

"Huh?" Spud replied.

"Back! Go back!" the raven screamed in his ear. Spud barely heard him, but he got the idea. He spun around, rapped the others with the nobbeltynook to get their attention, and led them toward the border at a quick-march. The cliff where they had seen the three heads was now just a plain rocky hill with the stream flowing around it, across a broad meadow and into Spud's land. As they neared the border, Spud glanced at his feet. His shadow was back.

"Can you hear me, Brokenwing?" he asked as they crossed the furrow.

"Quite well, Your Spudship."

"Where are we? What kind of place was that?"

"A land of symbols, and no, I do not mean the round things musicians clang together. Everything there stands for something else, and nothing is what it seems to be. If we had gone any farther, we probably would have become symbols, too!"

"I have enough trouble just being me!" Spud said. "Let's plow our way loose from here!"

When Blossom was harnessed and ready at the border, Spud looked at the green land and thought aloud, "Do you think it would be too dangerous to take just a piece of that meadow down where the brook flows into my stream? It sure would make a nice little souvenir."

"A little symbolism won't hurt," Brokenwing said. "Just make sure you don't overdo it."

So Spud cut a new furrow and added a bit of meadow and a short length of brook to his lands. Blossom would find good grazing in the meadow and maybe give symbolic milk, which sounded a little weird, but interesting.

What was the reason for coming to this place? Not a single living thing had been added to his kingdom. Or so he thought.

Early the next morning Spud strolled down to the fog bank to look at his new meadow and brook. Apparently, Blossom liked symbolic grass, for she was grazing happily. The day was already warm and the sky overhead a clear, cloudless blue. Spud sat by the brook, took off his boots and dabbled his feet in the water.

"Yeeeouch!" he cried. Something had bitten down hard on his big toe! He jerked his foot out of the water, and a fish came with it. It was long and pure white, with a red mark like a scar just behind the gills. It flopped around on the bank, but made no effort to regain the brook.

"So!" Spud said as he picked it up. "You thought my toe was a grub or a worm, did you? Do you know the penalty for biting the king's feet? Well, you're gonna become the king's breakfast, as soon as I can get you back to Gunnar! What do you think of that, my fine, finny friend?"

Spud did not expect a reply, but he held the fish up to his face to get a better look at it. The fish's mouth opened and closed rapidly several times, and then a faint, far-away-sounding voice seemed to come from it.

"Fresh water! Please! Quick!"

Chapter Sixteen

In which Spud finds a new love, loses an old friend,
and meets an old enemy
· · · · · · · · · · · · · · · · ·

Spud was so shocked that he nearly dropped the fish. He managed to hold on and ran for the cottage as fast as he could, shouting for his subjects as he went. The fish wriggled in his arms, and made no real effort to escape.

"What a beauty!" Gunnar cried when he saw the fish. "Hand it over and I'll have it cleaned and cooked for you in no time!"

"No! It's alive! It can talk! It needs fresh water! Quick! What have you got?"

Gunnar grabbed a small pail, poured in the spring water he had been using to soak some potatoes, and Spud dropped in the fish. The water barely covered it, and it had no room to swim. It twitched feebly to show it was alive.

"Did you say it talked?" asked an unbelieving Gunnar.

"Yes!" said Spud. "It asked for fresh water. Where can we keep it?" He thought for a moment, then snapped his fingers. "The springs! Malcolm, bring the spade from the shed. We'll dig out a pond for it. Brokenwing, do you know what kind it is?"

"Quark!" the raven answered. Spud held out his arm.

"Ouch! You bloodthirsty bird! You'd better have an answer! That one hurt!"

"It's a brook trout," the raven said as they hurried up to the old stump. "*Salvelinus fontinalis*. Most unusual! They are commonly speckled, but this one is pure white. Would you mind if I gave it a nip? I'd like to have a chat with it."

"I don't think so," Spud replied as Malcolm began to dig. "It's been through enough already. I'll do the talking with it. Do you think it's the reason we went to that strange land?"

"Most probably. It came from a land of symbols, so it must stand for something else. Let's see if we can find out what it really is."

The dirt flew as Malcolm dug. "Try to get water from all three springs!" Brokenwing urged.

"Just hurry!" Spud cried. The trout was about ready to turn belly up. Spud waited as long as he dared, then dumped it in the new pond. "Careful with the spade!" he added as the half-giant continued to shovel out the dirt.

The trout revived and began swimming around its new pond even as Malcolm Woolybottom enlarged it. Spud waited till Malcolm had finished. He then leaned over the bank, put his face in the water, and asked, "Who are you?"

The fish rose to the surface, stuck its mouth out of the water and said, "Right now I'm a trout. But usually I'm the Princess Fianola of Conn."

"Was that the land where I found you?" Spud frowned as he asked. The memory of that land was unpleasant.

"No, that is not my land," answered Princess Fianola the Fish. "I was taken there by a cruel sorcerer who kept me a prisoner in the brook until I agreed to marry him."

A chill passed over Spud. A sorcerer. . . could it possible be. . . ? "Was this sorcerer also known as the tempter?" he asked.

"Indeed, yes," the fish princess answered. "He never would have succeeded with my father, who is a good and righteous man. I was on a visit to my uncle when it happened, and he was weak and easily tempted."

"Who is your uncle?" Spud asked.

"You probably never heard of him," said the fish. "He's just a small, unimportant count in a small, unimportant kingdom. His name is Rolph."

"I know him, all right! He and his tempter friend tricked my poor brothers into leaving home and kidnapped Ma. He wanted our land. . .the land I'm standing on and your swimming in right now!"

"I know," said the fish. "I overheard them one night. My uncle would get your land when he gave me up to the tempter, but Uncle Rolph was afraid of what my father would do when he found out. The tempter said his magic would protect Uncle Rolph. He even offered to have Father killed and his throne given to Uncle Rolph!"

"And that conniving old skunk agreed?"

"No," said the fish. "Even Count Rolph would have no part in the murder of his own brother. But taking a poor family's land? He wouldn't lose any sleep over that!"

"Do you think she's telling the truth?" Spud asked Brokenwing.

"Well," said the raven, "there is a way to test her. If she really is a princess, she will be able to resume her true form for a few moments if a king requests it. You now qualify as a king, so you may ask her." His voice dropped to a hoarse bird whisper. "Be polite and ask her nicely," he warned.

"Uh, you're a right pretty trout," Spud said to the fish. "Could I please see you as a princess, just for a little bit?"

The fish princess hesitated. "Two men, a giant, and a raven are staring at me," she objected. "Right now I'm a fish and it doesn't bother me. But if I become a princess, I won't have any clothes on, and this pond is very shallow!"

Spud could see the justice in her objection. "Gunnar, hand me your cloak," he commanded. The Viking-turned-cook took off his thick, dark cloak and gave it to Spud, who spread it over the surface of the pond. The fish princess swam beneath it. Then the water heaved and a huge bubble formed under the cloak. It burst and the most beautiful face Spud had ever seen peered out at him. He was sure it was the girl he had glimpsed at Count Rolph's.

"Now do you believe me?" she asked.

"Um. . . er. . . ah. . . that is. . . Yes! Yes I. . . I do!" Spud stammered.

"Good!" said Princess Fianola. "I'm glad that's cleared up." The water rolled and heaved once more and another bubble formed. When it popped, the cloak lay flat on the water, and a white trout swam out from beneath it.

"How do I get her to become a full-time princess?" Spud asked. "She'd make a dandy queen, but I can't marry a trout!"

"Easy to answer, but not so easy to do," Brokenwing responded. "You must prove your love by overcoming the tempter and giving your blood to the princess."

"Thanks for making me feel good," Spud said bitterly. "I thought I was going to have to do something *really* difficult."

"It *will* be difficult, but not impossible," the raven answered. "Or you could say it will be impossible, but not difficult. Which would you prefer?"

"That don't make any sense at all! How can something be impossible but not difficult?"

"It's impossible to defeat the tempter *if* you fight him on his terms. I found that out, to my sorrow. Fight him on your terms instead, and you can win easily."

"How can I do that?" Spud said.

"Know exactly what you believe in, what is right and what is wrong. That's called having principles. Then stick to them, no matter what else is convenient or what else is popular. As I said, it's easy to say, but very hard to do."

"But you fought him and lost," Spud said. "I'm not a wizard. I'm not even a real king! I'm just. . . well. . . nobody, really."

"No! You are much more than that!" Brokenwing replied. "You defeated a Viking in battle and spared him. You rescued a small giant and overcame a big one. Yes, he was a false giant, but you were ready to fight him before you knew that. You outwitted captains in two different armies, saved a girl from a wolf and escaped from a mermaid. You've made some good laws and kept your kingdom peaceful. Don't fear the tempter! He should fear you!"

"Well, when are we gonna meet up with him again?"

"Soon," Brokenwing guessed. "You escaped him at Count Rolph's, at Grandma's cottage and the stream. Each time it strengthened you and weakened him. Now you've raided his own land and taken the Princess Fianola. He must be desperate. He will want to meet you as soon as he can."

Spud was still worried. It was one thing to meet an enemy he could see face to face. The tempter never came out and showed his true self. Instead, he hid himself in other people or creatures and had them do the evil for him.

"How can the tempter hide himself in others?" he asked.

"They let him," said the raven. "They expose a weakness, and the tempter takes it over."

"But how?"

"I'll tell you a story," Brokenwing offered. "A bird flew over a castle wall and dropped two seeds from its beak. One fell on smooth, polished stone and could find no place to sprout. So it withered and died. The other fell into a crack between two stones, where a little dirt and some moisture had gathered. It sprouted and took root. No one noticed because it was just a tiny plant in a big wall, but it grew and grew until the pressure from its growing began to split the stones. In time, it destroyed the entire wall."

"I never thought of Count Rolph as a wall," Spud remarked.

"He was not a bad man to begin with," said the raven. "He had many weak spots. The tempter dropped a seed into one and it grew. That seed was greed, and there are others."

"What will he try to drop into me?" Spud asked.

"I don't know," Brokenwing said. "You will have to look into your own soul to answer that."

Spud thought about this as he walked beside the stream with Gunnar. Where was he weak? Where would the tempter attack him? What disguise would he come in? And where would the kingdom wind up next?

Gunnar suddenly broke in on his thoughts. "Listen! Did you hear that?"

"Hear what?" asked a startled Spud. He listened, but could hear nothing but the lapping of water against the bank and the song of a bird somewhere over in Hood's Woods.

"Singing!" Gunnar cried. "The most beautiful singing I've ever heard!"

"I don't hear it," Spud replied. "Is it your imagination or. . ."

The realization hit suddenly. "Gunnar! Beware! It's a mermaid!"

"It can't be! I'm an old fighter who has seen too many battles. They want the young and the good like you. Only the Queen of the Mermaids herself, who has lived for thousands of years, would call to an old blood shedder like me!" His eyes widened in fear. . . or perhaps it was hope. "Do you think. . . can it be. . . I have found favor with the Mermaid Queen herself?"

Spud could still hear nothing, but Gunnar was now striding along the bank toward the shore. His eyes were fixed straight ahead and his feet seemed scarcely to touch the ground. Spud had to run just to keep up with him.

Spud's first thought was to stop him. One good thwack with the nobbeltynook would drop even a Viking in his tracks. Spud reached for it, then had another thought.

Was that what the tempter wanted him to do? Gunnar had been a loyal servant, though his heart belonged to the sea. Spud sometimes saw him trying to see beyond the fog as he gathered the morning's supply of fish. When the kingdom touched land and the fog disappeared, Gunnar spent his spare time gazing out where the water met the sky, looking. . . for what?

Something had touched Gunnar's soul. Maybe he was foolish. Maybe the tempter was using him. Ma had let Will and Tom go when the tempter called to them. It was Gunnar's fate, and Spud knew he must leave him to it.

"Go!" he said. "I release you!"

The Viking reached the fog bank and waded into the sea. Spud heard only the splash of water as Gunnar struck out swimming, then one high, faint note and everything was quiet. Gunnar-the-Washed passed from the story.

"Goodbye, Gunnar!" Spud called to the empty sea. "I hope she makes you happy! You deserve at least that!"

Later he asked Brokenwing if he had done the right thing.

"I believe you did," said the bird. "A servant kept against his will is a poor servant, indeed. Others will come in his place, and if the Queen of the Mermaids did call to him, she will remember and be grateful to you for letting him go."

They walked back to the cottage where Spud saw the Viking's great battle-ax lying beside the stove. "Should I throw it into the sea after him?" he asked.

"No," said Brokenwing. "By now he has either drowned or found a home with the mermaids. . . or perhaps both. In any case, he has no further need of weapons."

"I now have need of a cook," Spud said. "Running a kingdom and fixing meals for myself and a hungry giant takes a lot of time!"

"The mother of Juan the Youngest is an excellent cook," the raven told him. "If she were to come down here from the Spanish village, she could keep house for you and be close to her son and daughter-in-law as well."

"Then I'll make a law, just to be fair, that the mother of any new bridegroom can have the chance to work as cook and housekeeper for the king. How's that for a law, Brokenwing?"

"It's, ah, certainly unusual, Your Spudship."

So it was that the mother of Juan the Youngest became Cook and Housekeeper for King Spud, and Malcolm Woolybottom used the great battle-ax to chop kindling for her. After one day Spud had to admit that she was a far better cook than Gunnar or even Ma.

Two days later the fog began to lift again. Spud summoned Malcolm, Brokenwing, and Juan the Youngest for a council.

"I think we're heading for trouble," he told them. "This here tempter feller is up to something out there, and we've lost our only skilled fighter."

"With Blossom and the plow, we can always cut ourselves free again as soon as we strike land," Juan said.

"I don't want to do that," Spud replied. "If we run from danger, it'll just keep after us. Right, Brokenwing?"

"Fleeing from evil only makes it stronger," the raven agreed. "Whatever we have to face, we must face it in the land that lies beyond that fog." He looked out at the horizon and added, "And the fog will not be with us much longer!"

The kingdom rotated gently as the fog thinned. The meadow from the Land of Symbols would strike the new land. The new country looked familiar. "Brokenwing!" Spud cried. "Are we. . . ?"

"We are, indeed!" said the raven. "Look over there!"

On the shore of the new land stood a company of troops drawn up to meet them. At their head, mounted on a magnificent horse, sat a man in the robes of a king. Beside him, on a very ordinary horse, was a man Spud recognized at once.

It was Count Rolph!

Chapter Seventeen

*In which Spud tries single-handed combat and diplomacy,
Malcolm sets a record in knight-throwing, and Juan plays
customs agent*

· · · · · · · · · · · · · · · ·

"The count sure don't look happy," Spud observed.

"I suspect that is because the king does not look happy,"
the raven replied. "Look closely."

Spud's kingdom had drawn near enough for him to see
figures clearly. "Why, Old Rolph's all tied up! Why is that?"

"I think we'll soon find out!" Brokenwing said.

The two lands bumped together with a gentle earthquake
that made the king's horse rear and plunge, but the king kept
his seat. Count Rolph was not so lucky. His horse threw him
and bolted. No one offered to pick him up, so he lay where he
fell.

"How did they know we were coming?" Spud asked.

"The tempter has been at work again," the raven answered.
"Beware, Your Spudship! An angry king is a dangerous friend
and an even more dangerous foe!"

Spud's eyes narrowed and matched the king's glare for
glare. "I'm a king now myself, and I'm not gonna be scared
of anybody else!" he said.

"You!" the king shouted. "Who are you and how dare
you trespass upon my most glorious land?"

"My name is King Spud, and I ain't on your land! Everything on this side of the line belongs to me!" Spud replied.

"Everything I claim is mine, and I claim that miserable land of yours!" cried the king.

"Ain't your own land big enough already? But if you don't want us around, I'll cut us loose and we'll be on our way."

"I forbid that!" roared the king. "You are my subjects now, and you will do as I say!"

"Don't think he's the sort of feller I'd like for a neighbor," Spud muttered. "Claim and forbid all you want," he shouted to the king. "It's still my land, and I plan to keep it!"

The king sat absolutely still. Spud watched his face change from white to gray to black, like a cloud getting set to bust a thunderstorm loose. Before the storm broke, Spud said, "Can't say as I think very much of your army, if you need all them to handle the three of us. Anybody brave enough to fight me one-to-one?"

The king pointed to one of his knights. "Gullivan! Teach that young upstart a lesson!" he commanded.

"Fight a common peasant?" asked the knight. "He is not even mounted. Sire, let me send a foot soldier to deal with him."

"Shucks!" said Spud. "If that's all that bothers you, I'll get myself mounted. Malcolm, bring Blossom over here."

Spud hopped on the cow's back and brandished the nobbeltynook. I just wish Will was here to see this, he thought as he said to the knight, "There! You satisfied now?"

Apparently, Gullivan was satisfied, for he drew his sword and spurred his horse forward. Blossom stood chewing her cud as she watched him come. The knight swung with the flat of the blade, intending to knock Spud from the cow and stun him. But Spud caught the blow on his shield, and the sword rebounded like a ball thrown against a wall.

"Not as easy as you thought, is it?" Spud snickered.

Gullivan wheeled his horse and charged again. This time he swung with the sharp edge out, but again Spud caught the blow on his shield and the blade bounced away without causing damage. Nor did the force of the blow dislodge Spud, though he sat on Blossom's back with no saddle or stirrups.

This would almost be fun, if he wasn't trying so hard to kill me, Spud thought as the knight wheeled his horse again. So far, Spud had made no effort to hit back. This time, however, the knight charged his right side, away from the shield arm. "Reckon I'm gonna have to whack him this time," Spud muttered to himself.

The knight swung first. Spud parried the blow with the nobbeltynook and felt a slight tingle as the two weapons clashed. Gullivan's sword snapped in half, and before the astonished knight could ride clear, Spud rapped him on the side of his head. Gullivan dropped the broken sword and toppled from the saddle. His horse bolted back over the border.

"Pick him up and throw him back," Spud commanded Malcolm. "I ain't keeping nothing that belongs to that ugly old so-and-so!" The half-giant picked up the unconscious knight and casually tossed him over the heads of the king and his troops and into the top of a tree fifty feet behind them.

"Anybody else want to try his luck?" Spud asked.

The king pointed to another knight. "Cuthburt! Kill him!"

Cuthburt lowered his lance and charged. Spud leaned forward, took the point on his shield and snapped the lance with a blow from the nobbeltynook. Cuthburt was game enough. He dropped the broken lance and reached for his sword. But before he could draw, Spud whacked him and laid him out. Malcolm Woolybottom picked him up and threw him back over the border, over the king's troops and into another treetop sixty feet behind them.

"Look here now!" Spud called out as the king tried to pick another champion. "This is getting to be mighty hard on your army. I don't really like whacking 'em around, and Malcolm here might miss the treetops next time. Why don't we get together and have ourselves a chat, one king to another? Maybe we can work things out."

"Are you offering a truce?" the king asked.

"Guess you could call it that. We can go up to my Royal Cottage and Juan's ma can cook us up a mess of fish 'n beans 'n spuds. Don't know about you, but this fighting's made me kinda hungry!"

"Is this some kind of knavish trickery?" the king asked.

"Not on my part," said Spud. "Bring three or four of your men, if it'll make you feel better, but we need to have a chat. I know a few things that you'd like to know, and I'll bet you can answer some questions that have been giving me a blue botheration lately."

So Spud, Malcolm, Brokenwing, the king and three of his bodyguards marched to Spud's cottage to hold formal negotiations. Juan had run on ahead to tell his mother to get lunch ready. Count Rolph remained on the ground where he had fallen.

"Pull up a chair, King," Spud said as he seated himself at an old table made from the old tree. "Lunch should be ready in about two shakes." The king frowned, but sat.

"Be careful, Your Spudship!" Brokenwing warned. "You have never before tried statecraft or diplomacy. Always remember to think twice before you speak once."

"Don't worry," Spud murmured to the bird. "I can be just as nice as anybody. Watch this!" He turned to the king and said, "Now then, King. Why don't you just take off your boots, sit back and tell me what's put such a thistle burr in your britches?"

The king scowled and his face quivered like a pudding about to boil over. "You have taken something that belongs to me!" he said in a voice that fairly vibrated with rage.

"You mean this here land? Naw, King! This was Ma's land before old Count Rolph kidnapped her. All right, maybe I took some of his land, too. But he deserved it for being such a mean old sneak! Besides, I left him a lake that I bet looks right pretty!"

"I don't care a fig about the lake or the land!" the king shouted. "You have taken the Princess Fianola of Conn, who was pledged to me! Do you dare deny that?"

Spud was shocked, but managed to stare right back at the king. "Who told you this here princess was running around with me anyhow?" he asked.

"Count Rolph himself!" answered the king. "He said you stole her along with the land. He claims he tried to stop you, but you had a powerful sorcerer helping you and thwarted him with evil magic."

"He said that, huh?" Spud replied. "Well, let me tell you Count Rolph is a dad-burn liar! *He* was the one with the evil wizard. He tricked my poor, simple brothers into leaving home and then stole Ma. He'd have grabbed me and this here land, too, if I'd have let him!"

"Do you mean to say you have never seen nor heard of the Princess Fianola?" the king demanded.

"Well, King. I'm gonna be honest. I *did* meet up with a princess by that name. But it weren't in your kingdom. It was in a strange land we visited more'n a week ago. Or maybe it was years ago. Time works kinda funny around here."

"And she is with you now?" the king asked.

"Well, kind of. You see, right now she's a fish."

"What!" the king shouted.

"Now there's no need to get all riled," Spud said. "She's a perfectly good fish and in no danger, although I did almost eat her for breakfast once."

The king glowered at Spud. "Are you saying you turned my intended bride into a fish?" he demanded.

"Naw, King. I sure didn't," Spud replied.

The king grew thoughtful. "If you didn't, and Count Rolph didn't, then who did?" he wondered.

"Reckon it was that feller called the tempter," Spud replied. "I've had dealings with him. He turned my best advisor into a crippled bird, and he's been after me ever since I left your land. By the way, King. How did you know I was coming back? I didn't know where I was till I saw you and Count Rolph. And how come the count's all tied up?"

"A storyteller came to my palace a few weeks ago. He told me how you had stolen the count's land after you and he had plotted to kidnap Princess Fianola. He said you had a powerful wizard who worked evil magic, but the magic would fail when your land touched mine."

"Well, I ain't got any wizard around these parts," Spud said. "Just this here crippled bird and a half-giant and my

cow and my subjects. And the fish. Wanta go have a look at
her? Lunch can wait."

"Indeed, yes!" said the king. "Lead on!"

Spud set Brokenwing on his shoulder, and they hiked over
to the pond. "I feel the tempter's presence," the raven murmured. "He's not in you or the king, but he's around here
somewhere."

"You mean that old king's just nasty that way by nature?"
Spud asked. "Well, who else would be interested in a fish?"

"Meow!"

Old Tom crouched at the edge of the pond and poked at
the fish with a forepaw. The trout managed to stay just out of
reach. The cat was so intent on his prize that he didn't notice
Spud until he reached down and grabbed the cat by the loose
fur on his neck.

Usually when Old Tom was caught doing something
wrong, he either went limp while Ma or Spud scolded him or
else meowed an apology. But this time he came up spitting
and snarling. Spud was so startled he almost dropped him,
but he managed to hold the cat with one hand, while the other
reached for the nobbeltynook.

"You've got a mean spirit in you today, Old Feller," he
said, and rapped the cat right between the ears.

Old Tom went as limp as an empty sack, and Spud heard
the same rushing sound he had heard at Grandma's house.
This time, though, it was softer and fainter, as if the spirit
was losing power. Then the cat opened his eyes and meowed
to be put down. Spud set him on the ground, and Tom began
grooming his fur as if nothing had happened. The king, meanwhile, stared at the fish as it continued to swim around the
pool. "Is this really the Princess Fianola?" he asked.

"It sure enough is!" said Spud. "She can change back for
a quick little bit if a true king asks her to and she's agreeable.
But she's kinda shy about it, so I ain't asking her."

"Then I shall change her back," said the king. He looked
at Spud and finally managed a smile, although it took great

effort. "Then, if what you say is true, I will reward you by letting you go your way in peace."

Spud was itching to rap the king between the ears, just as he had done with the cat. But Brokenwing whispered, "No, Your Spudship. Let him try, for I think he will fail."

So Spud simply nodded. The king pointed to the fish and cried, "Fish! I command you to return to your rightful form as the Princess Fianola!"

Nothing happened. The fish continued to swim in circles.

"Do you hear me?" shouted the king. "You are to resume your rightful shape! Immediately! Right now! This very instant!"

The fish continued swimming. If the fish had heard the king at all, it paid no attention.

"This is a fraud!" declared the king. "You have tricked me, and you shall pay for it!"

"Hold your britches!" said Spud. "I'll show you how it's done." He spread Gunnar's cloak on the water and said, "Princess, could you please swim under there and show us your true self for a moment or two?"

The fish swam under the cloak and the bubble formed. When it burst, and the face of Princess Fianola looked up at them. "Thank you for being so polite," she said to Spud. Then the bubble formed again. When it popped, the fish swam back out.

"You see?" said Spud. "Some kings have the knack and some kings don't! I reckon she doesn't care for you that much. Or does it mean you're not really a true king?"

That was too much for the king. He snatched the crown from his head and threw it down in a rage. "You!" he cried. "You. . .you. . ."

Then he yanked a knife from his sleeve and struck. The blow was so swift and sudden that Spud couldn't react quickly enough to dodge. He managed to twist just enough so that the thrust missed his heart and jabbed his side instead. Spud lost his balance and tumbled backwards into the pond.

For a moment everyone stood as frozen as statues. Malcolm recovered his senses first. With a roar, he grabbed the king with one powerful arm and lifted him high over his head. "That's not nice!" he growled, and threw the king halfway back to the cottage. The bodyguards started to draw their swords, took one look at Malcolm's face and changed their minds about fighting. They ran to their king where he had landed and picked him up again.

Spud's eyes closed when he hit the pond. He sank straight to the bottom and couldn't find the strength to stand. He knew the water wouldn't even reach his waist if he could get to his feet, but his arms and legs seemed paralyzed. I'm going to drown in less than three feet of water, he thought.

Then he felt arms close around him and lift. His head broke the surface and his eyes opened again. Princes Fianola, wrapped in Gunnar's old cloak, was holding him up!

"Reckon it's my turn to thank you!" he said as soon as he could catch his breath.

"No," she replied. "I'm thanking you again. You broke the spell and freed me."

"How did I do that?"

"The tempter himself told me:
'Nevermore can you be free
Till a true king gives his blood to thee!'

"I could understand how a king might shed his blood *for* me," she continued. "But how could he give his blood *to* me? When you fell in the pond, you bled in the water and I took it in through my gills! So now I am free from the spell!"

"But we ain't free yet!" Spud said. "Where's that sneaky king anyhow? It was downright nasty of him to stick me that way!"

"He's out cold and they're carrying him back to the border," Brokenwing said. "As soon as he comes to, he will order a general attack. We must plow ourselves free before he recovers!"

"Malcolm! Get Blossom and let's get to it!" Spud ordered.

Juan had already harnessed the cow in case they needed a quick getaway. Malcolm ran to get Blossom while Juan and Princess Fianola helped Spud out of the pond.

"Are you strong enough to do it?" Juan asked.

"Don't matter," said Spud. "I'm the only one who *can* do it!" He picked up the crown the king had hurled down in his anger and placed it on his head. It fit perfectly. "If I'm gonna act like a king, I might as well look like one," he added. "Now help me get to the border."

They reached the furrow just before the bodyguards arrived with the still-unconscious king. "Halt!" Spud cried weakly. "Before you recross my border, you must make a declaration to my customs officer." He turned to Juan and whispered, "Hold them up until I get plowing. If they get him back in their own land and bring him to, he'll order his army to kill us all!"

Juan tried to remember how the Spanish and Moorish officials had acted. "Are you carrying any contraband out of this land?" he asked in as stern a voice as he could manage.

"No, just our king," a soldier replied.

"He doesn't look much like a king. Where's his crown?"

"Your king took it, as you well know," said the soldier.

Meanwhile, Spud, with Malcolm's help, had set the plowshare in the furrow and quietly urged Blossom forward.

"That's a serious charge!" Juan said. "Did you fill out the proper forms?"

"We don't have to. We're not your subjects. Now let us pass!"

The unconscious king began to stir and groan. The soldiers carrying him shifted their weight from foot to foot and looked very impatient. Juan looked beyond them and saw Spud slowly drawing the plow along the furrow. If he could stall them just a few moments more. . .

Spud had to use all his strength to hold the plow steady. His legs moved like he was wading through chest-deep water. He could feel the blood running down his side and knew he should lie down and have the wound bandaged before he bled to death. Unless he cut the land free, though, he would die anyway, and all his friends would die with him.

He decided to take a shortcut and sacrifice part of the meadow of symbols. Blossom swung left at his command and began to cut a new furrow. . .

"I suppose we can give you permission to leave," Juan said as he watched Spud cut the line. "Do you plan to come back soon? Would you recommend this land to your friends?"

At this point, the king came to his senses and growled, "Get me out of here! Prepare to attack! Spare the princess, if she is human, but kill everyone and everything else!"

Spud looked over his shoulder and watched them leave. The instant they crossed the new furrow, he urged Blossom forward with all his remaining strength. He felt the earth tremble beneath him and knew he had completed the cut. As his kingdom pulled free from the mainland, King Spud fell on his face and lay still.

Chapter Eighteen

In which Spud meets an old friend in a new form, finds Ma and hears a most amazing duet
· · · · · · · · · · · · · · · ·

When Spud finally opened his eyes, he was lying on his bed. His arms and legs seemed to have no strength at all. He could feel the gentle up-and-down motion of the land and knew they were adrift in time and space again.

"We made it then!" he mumbled. "We got loose!"

"We did, indeed!" said a voice he knew well. Spud looked around. Brokenwing wasn't there. A tall, thin man dressed in gray and white robes stood before him.

"Who are you?" Spud asked.

"I was once a bird with a broken wing," the man answered. "But your last triumph broke the spell, so now I am myself again."

"What do I call you now?" Spud wondered.

"I rather like the name you gave me, Your Spudship. It reminds me of what can happen when wizards get too proud of their powers. Feel free to call me Brokenwing whenever I'm in your land."

"Are you leaving us?"

"For a while," the wizard said. "You are not the only young man struggling against fate and temptation. There are many of you and precious few of us. I'll try to return from time to time."

"I'll miss you, Brokenwing."

"There is someone here to take my place," the wizard

said. "Two someones, in fact. I believe they have some bread and tea for you." Then, raising his voice, he added, "He's awake now."

The Princess Fianola was even more beautiful than he remembered. Pretty as she was, however, it was the person with her who caused Spud to drop his jaw in disbelief.

"Ma! What are you doing here?" he cried.

"I've been here all the time," she said. "The tempter couldn't take me from the land by force, so he took the cow instead and transformed me to take her place. He was planning to trick you into selling me."

"When the tempter realized how tough you all were, he betrayed Count Rolph to the king and grabbed the princess for himself," the wizard explained. "But she, too, was tougher than he thought and wouldn't give in. Therefore, he changed her into a fish and hid her in his own land while he hunted us through time and space."

Spud managed a weak laugh. "You mean, while he was roaming the world for us, we were right in his own land?"

"Yes, the very last place he thought to look. When you took part of his land and the princess, it weakened him so much that all he could control was your cat. When you spared the cat and drove him out, it finished him and broke his power over me."

"So there will be no more temptation?" Spud asked.

"Well, Your Spudship. You simply defeated *one* tempter, and a very minor one at that. There are many, many others. We have won a small battle, but the war goes on."

"Can you send us someone to run the church?" Spud asked.

"I will see what I can find," Brokenwing said. "There was a Welsh monk who put out to sea in a small boat a few centuries ago. Perhaps I could go back in time and pick him up before he drowned."

"As long as he can perform a wedding," said Spud as he smiled at the princess.

After tea and a nap, Spud felt strong enough to get up. Ma and Princess Fianola supported him as they walked down toward the stream. Blossom, the real Blossom, grazed peacefully, while Malcolm Woolybottom helped Juan the Youngest and the daughter of Han Lo in the field. As they neared the fog bank, Spud stopped.

"Listen!" he cried. "Do you hear it?"

"Hear what?" asked the princess. Ma shook her head.

"Singing! Like a mermaid. . . but not just a mermaid. It's a duet! Someone with a horrible off-key bass. . . like a drunken Viking!"

"Could it be Gunnar?" Ma wondered. "He was right nice to me when I was a cow!"

Spud knew then he had been right in letting the Viking go. If Gunnar had been with them at the last encounter, he would have charged into the king's army and started a fight that would have got them all killed. As it was, he was happy, and this was his way of telling them.

"Let's go home," Spud said. He turned away from the sea as the fog settled thickly around the rim of his island, and the Kingdom of Messy Potatoes drifted through time and space.

Chapter Nineteen

*In which the storyteller reaches an ending
and the story begins once again*
· · · · · · · · · · · · · · · · ·

Grandfather knew he would not last the year. My visits became day trips. Dad would bring me up on Saturday mornings, leave me with Grandfather Kneale for a couple of hours and then take me home in the afternoons. But while I was there, we worked hard on the story.

"I had no idea what was going to happen when I began," he told me once. "So now I have to go back over it in my mind and try to fit the pieces together. Let me read you what I have."

Then he read to me, slowly, in a voice that grew fainter each time I came. I wondered how he wrote it, until Mrs. Phelps told me two of his former students took turns coming over and writing it down as he dictated to them. I had to read the last two chapters to him, but we discussed them, just as we had the others, and he always asked for my suggestions.

My last visit came on Memorial Day, 1989. We finished the last chapter, and he held out his hand to me. I took it, but he didn't have strength enough to squeeze. I just held it for a while and finally said, "I love you, Grandfather."

"I love you too, Son," he answered.

That was the last time I saw him alive. He called us sometime in June and asked to speak to me. I had to listen real hard, because he couldn't talk louder than a whisper by then.

"I dreamed I saw Hugh last night," he said. "It was so real that I wonder if it was a dream. He told me he loved me and said everything would be all right. He said to tell you he thinks you're okay too. He says you're a lot like him and Spud, and he hopes you find your kingdom someday."

That was all. Grandfather Kneale went into a coma in late July and died on August 2, 1989. I remember the date because exactly one year later Saddam Hussein invaded Kuwait and the standoff known as Desert Shield began. In January, 1991, Desert Shield became Desert Storm, and in February General Schwarzkopf's troops took the Iraqis apart in a war that lasted a hundred hours.

All the boys in the school (and a lot of the girls too) walked around all puffed and proud that we had kicked Hussein's butt so easily. But I thought about Grandfather's friend, Professor Jamal, and his son who wanted to come to America to study. He had been drafted, instead, into the Iraqi army. Was he one of the enemy we were so happy to have blown away?

By the time Desert Storm was fought, Grandfather's house had been sold, torn down and a new apartment complex built on the lot. I was sad that the house was gone, yet relieved that no one else would take over the place that had been so special to Grandfather and me. I can still close my eyes and see it in my mind just as it was on the day I first went there.

Grandfather left a lot of his money to the church, some to Mom and a little to Mrs. Phelps. He also set up a trust fund to pay for college for Martha Ann and me. He set up a college fund for Jason, too. Mrs. Phelps broke down and cried when she heard about it.

Before the house was sold, Mom and I went through it and took a few special things to remember Grandfather by. I chose the big globe he had first used to show me where Mesopotamia was. We also saved several cartons of his books. "Good books should be read more than once," he had said.

I also took the picture of Uncle Hugh, which I still have. There was one thing, however, I wanted more than any other.

It wasn't in his house. I secretly knew I would get it some day and, finally, I did.

Two extra packages came for Christmas in 1991. There was a big one with Mom's name on it and a smaller one for me. Mom insisted they be the last ones opened, and I knew then what they were. Hers was a big book bound in leather. On the front, stamped in gold, was the title: *The Kings of Mesopotamia*. Below that, in smaller letters were the words, Rev. Ehric Kneale, D.D., Ph.D.

My book was smaller, but a lot more interesting. I ripped off the wrapping and saw on the cover a picture of a boy sitting astride a cow, holding a wooden shield, and brandishing a weird club made from an old tree root. A raven with a bandaged wing sat on his shoulder, and a half-giant and a Viking stood on each side. The boy looked a lot like Hugh and me. Grandfather must have sent the artist a picture.

At last! *The King of Messy Potatoes!* "Look on the dedication page," Mom urged.

I turned past the title page and read:

For my two boys

Hugh Michael Kneale
&
John Kneale Brooks

Martha Ann said, "Dook! Dook!" and made a grab for it, but I held it up out of reach. For once Mom did not urge me to share. "You can read it to her in a few years," she said. "But for now it's yours and nobody else touches it."

As she sat my sister down with one of her stuffed animals, I turned to the first chapter and began to read.

"Once upon a time, there was a boy named Spud. . ."

THE END